The Carmen Miranda Memorial Flagpole

*A Novel
by Gerald Rosen*

Presidio Press, California. 1977

Copyright © 1977 by
 Presidio Press
 1114 Irwin Street
 San Rafael, California 94901
Cloth Cover Edition ISBN: 0-89141-032-5
Paperback Edition ISBN: 0-89141-033-3
Library of Congress Catalog Card Number: 77-073554

Book design by Jon Goodchild
Cover design by Georgia George

Printed in the United States of America

For my parents
and for Marijke

I kept dreaming of Asiatic journeys, of going overland to China, of impossibilities, of the Indies or of California . . .

Gustave Flaubert

When you're in love, the whole world is Jewish.

Confucius

Psychiatric Introduction

Dear Reader,
   I am not a writer, but a physician—a psychiatrist in fact. I have taken on the task of preparing this unusual "psychiatric introduction" to warn against buying this book. In fact, I implore you not only not to buy it, but not to read it as well. I feel it is my duty to do this.
   The fact that I am being paid a modest amount by Gerald Rosen for doing this has not influenced me in the least. I will grant you that I did not refuse the money, but only because it has been my experience with patients on the couch (so to speak) that in this culture people only value what they pay for. It is for this reason, by the way, that a psychiatrist like myself is forced to charge what might appear to some people as relatively high fees. I understand quite clearly the, shall we say, "spiritual benefits" which would accrue to me if I attempted to treat my patients for moderate fees, but I cannot allow myself to follow this attractive path at the expense of my patients' welfare.
   But, to return to the matter at hand, it occurs to me that writing an introduction to a book in which one asks the reader *not* to buy the book in question is probably a rare, if not a unique, endeavor. Yet, in the present circumstances, I felt I could not do otherwise. You see, if I had the power to prevent the publication of this book, I would do so. Unfortunately, when I did have this power (when Rosen was an in-patient at the Sonoma County Mental Hospital), he acted in a manner which the layman would probably classify as that of a harmless crackpot, and, I admit it, he talked me into recommending that he be released on a year's probation, provided he came in to see me each week. In fact, he often did not show up for his appointments, giving as his excuse (probably true) that he was working on this book. This seemed a constructive enough activity, so I covered up for him. It wasn't until he was released from probation that he allowed me to read the manuscript. I then suspected I had made a mistake in his treatment.

I

Since then my suspicions have been more than confirmed. Actually, I was not to see him as a charity patient. In order to instill a sense of responsibility in him, I requested that he pay for his visits—which he never did, by the way. I let him get away with this, simply allowing his bill to mount up and only charging him six percent interest at a time when, if you recall, the prime rate charged by the biggest banks to their most reliable customers was over ten percent. And I would hardly call Gerald Rosen reliable. But, nonetheless, I felt I could act as a kind of half-way house between the hospital and the cold world that he would have to confront when he was cured. I had to teach him to pay his debts to society. Not to conform, necessarily, but simply to pay those obligations we all owe to each other if we are to continue to live in the urban megalopolis which we have created. It is for this reason, and for this reason alone, that I have put a lien on his royalties for this book.

(I don't like to digress, but it occurs to me that what I've said above should not be taken as a blanket approval of the urban megalopolis. You are, no doubt, familiar with the experiments in which rats exhibited bizarre behavior when kept in overcrowded conditions, and, after all, man *is* an animal.)

To get to the heart of the matter, I believe this book to be the product of a not-so-harmless crackpot. If it achieves any measure of success, I believe it may harm the society and, most important to me as a physician, it may harm my former patient, Gerald Rosen himself.

To be specific, you will notice that right at the beginning of this book, Mr. Rosen claims to be an accountant. Poppycock! Granted, by some study of accounting textbooks he can pass himself off within the novel (by using selective details and name dropping) as having a knowledge of accounting. But *a real accountant? Gerald Rosen?* By no means!

All right. I can anticipate your objections at this point. I am not unfamiliar with literary conventions. (In fact, when I was younger, I published a paper on literature—an analysis of Oedipal motivation in the Latvian novel—for which I read thirty novels in the original Latvian. The paper appeared in the *Journal of Baltic Sea Studies*, by the way, XVXI: 122-129, Je 7, 49.) So I know, quite well, that a narrator is not necessarily the author, but can be a character the author pretends to be—a voice he assumes through which to tell the story of an imaginary person interacting with other imaginary people in a more or less imaginary world. All right. So be it. Well and good.

But here's the difference. In my dealings with Gerald Rosen, I have come to see that he does not believe his characters are imaginary. He believes his work is autobiographical and that all the characters are, quite literally, real. And, alas, even worse for him, he behaves as if they were not merely sides of himself (the many facets of what, in most authors, would be an integrated personality), but he behaves as if they were actually living people interacting with the real world. Mind you, I said *behaves*, not fantasizes. And this is where his sickness lies.

As an example, he claims to have a twin brother, Jack, who is a writer. Well, this is false—a dissociative reaction on his part—a retreat into the fantasy that he is not a radical gadfly to the society, but a respectable accountant. Again, this is harmless enough. But here's the kicker (so to speak). I have actually seen him dressed as he describes his "brother," acting like his "brother," wearing that crazy hat with the fruit on it which he ascribes to his "brother," and getting into trouble like his "brother." (I had to get him out of jail several times in connection with such incidents as the Water Commission fiasco and the Safeway scandal which he describes in the text that follows.)

OK. Even this is understandable. He's lonely. He wants a brother. He fantasizes that a brother exists. And then he attributes his crazy pranks to his imaginary brother as a way of not facing up to what he himself has been doing. Alas, if only this were all.

You see, at different times he behaves like *each* of his characters. I have seen him in a suit and tie telling people he is Doctor Ernest Hemingberg, a teacher of creative writing. I have seen him in hippie garb, telling people he is Luigi (who, he claims in the novel, is his wife's brother). I have seen him on Market Street in San Francisco, wearing those "bum

III

clothes" that he owns and acting as if he were Angie the Janitor, another of his wife's "brothers." I have even seen him in jockey silks, claiming he was Rodney the Jockey whom he describes as his "father-in-law" in the novel which follows.

But Angie doesn't exist! Nor does Luigi! Nor does Rodney the Jockey. Nor, alas, (excepting his wife, Nectarine, and his son, Jimi) do most of the other characters in his novel who he insists are real, but whom, in spite of the most ardent investigative efforts (on my *days off!*), I have never been able to locate. In fact, to confuse matters even further, I have seen him at bars on San Francisco's Polk Street, dressed in drag, claiming he *was* Nectarine!

And if this weren't outrageous enough, one day I came into my office a bit late and I found him *in my chair*, beginning analysis on a new patient. He was claiming to be *me!* When I tried to reason with him, he threatened to have me locked up as a madman and a charlatan. Imagine! Me! A charlatan. Indeed!

And, alas, as this book goes to press, I must report that after several months of wearing clothes like mine and pretending to be me at several expensive Bay Area bars (and charging his drinks to me, no less!), he has changed his tack and has begun to tell these same people that, in fact, I, Dr. Samuel Freudenberg, do not exist and am merely a creature of his imagination. And that *he* wrote this introduction to his own book.

Balderdash! I do exist. This is my voice. I am a human being and I demand to be heard and to be acknowledged as such.

All right, I'll drop my professional demeanor. I'll get angry. I'm human too. I have to live with this guy's pranks. And I'll tell you why he's written this book, even if he himself is unaware of it. If you want my opinion, he's written this book as part of his efforts to destroy the notion of a single, integrated personality. I think he wants to increase his repertoire of imitations until he himself cannot remember who he really is. I think he wants to *be* Carmen Miranda. He wants to wear fruit on his head and dance on television. I think, in his mad despair, he unconsciously wants to destroy the very idea of sanity itself.

Now, as I said, I don't believe he is *consciously* doing this. He may not even remember doing his imitations when he wakes up the next morning. But conscious or unconscious, the effect is the same. So I beseech you, do not read any further. If you have already bought this book (and have resisted the temptation to underline some of the things I've said), please take it back to the bookstore for a refund. (You'll find many bookstores to be quite generous in this regard.) But I beg you, don't give him the means to indulge his mad fantasies and to besmirch my reputation any further. Or to challenge the very fact of my existence as a separate and distinct personality, quite different from the "Doctor Freudenberg" he portrays in his book.

I am, dear reader; I swear to you, I am. Pinch me, do I not hurt? Cut me, do I not bleed? Don't pay your bill to me, do I not sue? I am. I swear it. I am.

Dr. S. Freudenberg, M.D.

The Carmen Miranda Memorial Flagpole

Chapter 1

FOETEO ERGO SUM.
　I stink, therefore I am.
　Descartes had to be French, right? That's the problem with the French. Always putting Descartes before the horse.
　I thought I'd open with a joke. Loosen things up a bit, if you know what I mean. You see, I'm not a writer. I'm an accountant. It's my brother who's the writer. He's Jack. I'm Jerry. He's the one who should be writing this book. But he's not here right now.
　(Jack, if you're reading this, please come home. We miss you.)*

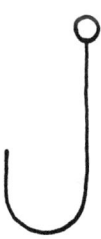

　That looks like a big "J" doesn't it? It's really a hook. Every

---

*Really! Do you see what I mean? And this is only the beginning. I warn you, get out while there's still time. Go to a movie.
　　　　　　　　　　　　　　　　　　　　　　　　　　Dr. F.

book has to have a hook, right at the beginning, to hold the reader's interest. My creative writing teacher, Dr. Ernest Hemingberg, told me that. He was a damn good teacher, old Ernie. But he was really paranoid. Kept going on about agents being after him. Trying to lock him up. I was really sorry that the class had to end when they put him in a mental hospital.

You ever read *Tonio Kroger?* By Thomas Mann? He says in there that an artist has to be part bourgeois. That's why I think I might be able to get this book together. I'm all bourgeois.

My brother Jack isn't bourgeois at all.

My brother and I grew up in The Bronx. In Highbridge. It was a pretty tough place, Highbridge. You may think your neighborhood is tough, but let me tell you how tough our neighborhood was. Our neighborhood was so tough that even Doberman pinschers would only go out on the streets at night in pairs. (Ratatatat—Bong!) No, seriously, though, our neighborhood really was tough. We had this guy on our block named "One-Eye" DeFortuna. How can I tell you how mean this guy was? OK. I got it. This guy was so mean that in World War Two, if the atom bomb didn't work, they were going to drop *him* on Hiroshima. (Ratatatat—Bong!) But, seriously, all I can say about One-Eye DeFortuna is that if losing an eye could make a guy that mean, I'd hate to ever run into him if he went blind.

Well, like I said, my brother and I were born in The Bronx. On December 24th. In the Royal Hospital on The Grand Concourse. Right after Hitler attacked Poland.

"The Grand Concourse!" That's a laugh. The name was probably "Schwartzfarb Avenue" or something, and then the landlords got together and changed it to "The Grand Concourse" and suddenly everyone's rent went up twenty bucks for living on such a fancy street.

Anyway, my parents were in the iron and steel business. My mother ironed and my father stole. (Ratatatat—Bong!) No, seriously, I apologize. I'll try to stop. I can't help it. I love old jokes. Jokes were the only art form we had in The Bronx.

But where was I? Did I tell you my brother and I were

twins? I guess you figured that out by now. We were born on the same day here on our dear old beloved planet Pesseema.

(You don't mind if I call you "folks" do you? It sure beats "Dear Readers" by a long shot. I'll save that "Dear Readers" crap for the shrink I invent to write the introduction to this book when I'm done.*)

So, let's see, I told you we're twins. Identical twins. Now whenever anyone meets us they look us over (like they were thinking of buying us) and then they say, "Hey . . . you guys twins or something?" And we have to smile and do our twin number. It's show biz, folks.

Anyway, I won't put the twin numbers in the book. Whenever we meet dumb people, you just fill in a twin number right at the start. Complete with, "Hey, Myra . . . C'mere for a sec . . . I got something to show ya . . . "

But I can hear old Ernie shouting at me from his padded cell: "Stop *telling!* *Show* them something already! Some dialogue. Some action. A little life, for Pete's sake."

OK, Ernie. You got a point there.

Let's get the show on the Cross-Bronx Expressway, folks. (Ernie, if you're reading this, we haven't forgotten you. We'll find you and get you out if it takes years. Keep up your hopes.)

OK. We're in New York. It's spring. The Jewish birds are flying back from Miami Beach where they spent the winter. The grass in the outfield in Yankee Stadium is turning green. The first intellectual appears on the steps of the public library on Fifth Avenue. The managers of the Orange Julius stands are beginning to smile again.

You know. Spring. In the Big Apple.

And we're there too. Me and my brother Jack. And our Great Dane dog, "Hark, the Herald Tribune Angels Sing." We call him "Hark" for short.

Anyway, we're going to California. In a covered station wagon. Pulled by 300 horses. Made by the Ford Motor Company.

*Ha, ha. Very funny! You should be on TV, you jerk!
　　　　　　　　　　　　　　　　　　　Dr. F.

Our wagon is going to be loaned to us by the You-Go-Drive-A-Car Service. Owned by a guy named You-Go Feltner. (Of the Flatbush Feltners.) Actually the guy spelled his name "Hugo," but my brother Jack immediately began to pronounce it "You-Go" and when Hugo and his wife didn't pick up on it, my brother kept it up. As a private joke. Just between the two of us. Like I said, we're twins. There's got to be some compensations for what we have to put up with.

So we get to Forty-second Street at eight o'clock in the morning. The day was so average I won't even try to describe it. My brother had gotten up when he was supposed to without a struggle. He leaped out of bed, shouting, "Get the station wagons in a circle! We're surrounded."

Hark wasn't with us. Only people were allowed to go in the station wagon. And six cartons of records weren't allowed to go either. The plan was for us to drive back to Grove Street in the Village where we lived; pick up Hark and the records; jam the rest of the space full with pots, pans, pillows, and whathaveyou; and give everything that wouldn't fit to our friends on the block. Then off to Jersey and points west. We'd already mailed the thirty cartons of books ahead of us.

The You-Go Service was on the eighth floor of an old office building just off Seventh Avenue. I know it couldn't have been Eighth Avenue because we won't go to Eighth Avenue since they tore the old Madison Square Garden down. "I wish the Germans had bombed it during World War Two. Then at least we'd know who to blame," my brother says.

Next door to the entrance to the building was a movie theater playing a double of *Junior High Madam* ("How far should a teacher go in educating her students?") and *Deep Nose.*

OK, we're in the elevator. Me and my brother Jack. He's thirty-one years old. Six feet tall, a hundred seventy-five pounds, dark hair that wants to be kinky but is only curly, sensitive mouth, large nose, slightly crooked since he was *tackled* trying to turn the corner in a football game (without equipment) against the Irish guys on the cobblestones of 170th Street, beautiful soft large brown eyes that diverge slightly and always seem to be asking questions of someone in the distance and light up his face with a hope that makes him seem almost painfully vulnerable and alive, over high wide cheekbones (from our Russian-Jewish father?). And a ruddy complexion.

I look that way, too.

("Ruddy complexion." That's a joke. Sounds like some new Hollywood star in the audience on the old Ed Sullivan Show: "Ruddy Complexion! Stand up and take a bow. Let's hear it, folks! For *Ruddy!*")

(The first time I heard that ruddy complexion business was when we went to our draft board. We were enlisting in the army. What it means is: "This cat had acne, in The Bronx, in the 1950s, and didn't kill himself. So let's give him a break and say his face is 'ruddy.' No one knows what it means anyhow.")

In the elevator with us there was this old priest. "Hi ya doin, father?" I said to him, and he smiled. I like priests. In The Bronx, if you could walk down the street near a priest the Irish guys wouldn't knock your teeth out that day. Of course I'm not Christian, though. That's one thing good about being Jewish. At least you don't have to be Christian.

The elevator stopped with a jerk. We saw the You-Go Service across the hall in Room 804. The door was open so we walked in. It wasn't the most beautiful setup I had ever seen. It looked like a Western Union office that had had its telegraph taken away.

Hugo and Clara were behind the counter. We'd met them the week before when we applied for the car. Hugo was short, fat, nervous. In his fifties. Jack tried to deal with him but Clara seemed to run things. Clara had a round face with painted-on, abstract expressionist eyebrows. Each of them was saying *something*, but it wasn't, "I'm really an eyebrow, folks."

She looks us over suspiciously.

"You boys are going to California?"

"That's right, Clara," Jack says.

"In the new Ford station wagon?"

"We're ready to go."

"Then where are your bags?"

Shit! She's got us. And we both know it. Jack's Adam's apple bounces like a hanged man at the end of his rope. But he quickly steps into the breech, as Henry the Boring Fifth would say. (The only breech we had in The Bronx was Orchard Breech on Long Island Sound, and that was so crowded and hot you never could really tell whether you were relaxing on the sand or were still packed in the damn bus that went there from Fordham Road.)

"Well . . . er . . . you see Clara . . . Did I ever tell you about my uncle Philly? The one from . . . er . . . Philly?"

"No."

"Oh . . . I thought I did . . . "

"The suitcases?"

"Oh, yeah . . . well . . . er . . . have you ever heard about the custom of the Matzocoatl Indians called a busk?"

"The Matzocoatl?" You-Go says.

"Yeah. They're these Indians in New Mexico."

"Some think they're one of the ten lost tribes of Israel," I add.

Jack smiles. We're working as a team now.

Jack says, "They live right near another tribe called the Overcoatls."

"Yeah," I say, "between them and the Trenchcoatls."

You-Go and Clara are confused. They really don't believe us, but they sense that we're educated so they're afraid to object. We've got em on the run.

"But seriously," I say, "you know what a busk is?"

"A busk?" Clara says.

"Yeah, a busk," Jack says.

"This ain't nothin dirty?" Hugo chimes in like a cracked bell.

"You-Go, please!" Jack says. "My brother is a C.P.A. We're not a couple of your Forty-second Street bums."

Clara throws Hugo a dirty look. Hugo apologizes with his tone as he mumbles to her, "Well, this is a *car* we're giving them, Boopie."

"Not pancakes," I add.

"Yeah, not pancakes," Hugo says.

"Boopie?" Jack says. *"Boopie?"*

Hugo and Clara blush. We've got them now. Don't fuck with a writer when it comes to words. That's his business. He'll hear each one. It's like trying to punch out a professional boxer in a bar. You're not gonna deck him with a lucky punch.

"Anyway," Jack continues, "my uncle Philly is an anthropologist."

"A student of the science of man," I explain.

"He is also very rich," Jack says. "He lived with the Matzocoatl for years."

"He *believes* in the Matzocoatl."

"And he offered to give us a thousand bucks apiece if, before we leave for California, we end this period of our lives in the Matzocoatl manner by performing a busk on all our possessions—which means burning them up in a kind of big bonfire."

"Which we did last night. In a big busk in Brooklyn."

"It was in the *Times*. You read the *Times?*" Jack asks Clara, whose very perfume exudes *Daily News*.

"No . . . I'm afraid I didn't this morning," she says.

"Well," Jack continues, "they said it was the biggest busk in Brooklyn since 1961 when a man named Greenblat was caught performing a busk on the heavily insured warehouse of his failing electrical supply company."

"Really . . . We should get going," I say, looking at my watch.

"You don't have anything against Indians, do you?" Jack asks Clara.

"No . . . Why should I have anything against Indians?"

"Yeah," Hugo adds, "why should we have anything against Indians?"

"Well," Jack says, looking at them suspiciously, "you never know . . . As for myself, I never met an Indian I didn't like."

"Me neither!" Hugo frogs in, adamantly.

Clara gives him a look that shuts him up.

"You-Go's right," Jack says. "I can see his point."

"After all, you can't be too careful," I say. "This is a *car* you're giving us."

"Not a bottle of Log Cabin Syrup," Jack says.

"OK, already," Clara says to Hugo, "go get them the car. And get me a danish on the way."

"Cheese or prune?" Jack asks.

"Oh . . . prune."

"You hear that, You-Go?" Jack says.

7

Hugo looks at him, puzzled. "She *always* takes prune."

"Good!" Jack says, in his best bedside manner. "Promotes regularity."

"Regularity in management is at the heart of sound business practice on any level," I say.

"I told you he was a C.P.A.," Jack says. "Now run along, You-Go. I'm sure Clara has other business to attend to."

"Yeah," Clara says. "What d'ya think, Hugo? I ain't got all day."

Hugo scurries out the door.

Chapter
2

FINALLY, AFTER FILLING OUT FORMS and getting instructions from Clara . . . ("Now you remember to send me a postcard every day so we can check your path on the map. And stay on the route. You're not insured if you go over fifty miles off it.") . . . we take the keys and try to leave.

Clara stops us. "Wait a minute, fellas. Hugo will go with you part of the way."

My brother and I exchange a quick look. We both see a picture of Hark waiting for us between the cartons of records in our naked apartment. While we may be driving across the swamps of Jersey in a few minutes with Hugo in the car.

Sure enough, Hugo plants himself in the rear seat and as we move off toward the Lincoln Tunnel he begins to talk about their office in Pittsburgh. And we're both sitting there hoping like crazy that he's just going to see us to the entrance of the tunnel.

But maybe he's going to Pittsburgh! With us!

PANIC!

Finally, at Eleventh Avenue, just before the entrance to the tunnel, Hugo says, "OK, boys. Pull over and let me out. I can watch from here."

Hugo derricks himself out of the car with a grunt. Before the door has a chance to close, Jack slams down on the gas and the wheels sing as we spin around the corner, running the red light, out into the traffic on Eleventh Avenue, leaving the tunnel behind.

But not poor fat Hugo. He spins out too and I look through the rear window and there he is, out in the middle of Eleventh Avenue, running like hell down the center of the street.

"Jack! Step on it! It's Hugo! He's chasing us!"

"What?"

"Move it, damn it! His feelings are wounded. He could be dangerous."

Jack tries to change lanes but he's boxed in by a city bus.

"Come on, Jack! *Move it!*"

Jack tries to see Hugo in the rear view mirror but his view is blocked by a van. I'm sticking my head out of my window.

"Step on it, Jack!"

"Are you kidding me?"

Jack tries to pick up speed but we're still boxed in.

"No. Come on. He's gaining! He just passed that Seven Santini Brothers' moving van. He's behind the green truck with the crates of live chickens on it."

The light changes. Red. We're trapped. Jack hits the horn but we can't move because thirty-four Puerto Rican guys are crossing the street in front of us, pushing racks of dresses. Jack spins his head around and spots Hugo steaming toward us. "Batten down the hatches!" Jack shouts. We scramble to roll up the windows and lock the doors. "Rig for silent running!"

Hugo puffs up and grabs the handle on Jack's door. When he sees it's locked, he blows his cool and begins to pound on the roof.

"Hugo!" Jack shouts. "This is a *car!* Not a fucking stack of pancakes!"

Hugo keeps pounding. Then he clutches madly at Jack's door handle. The thirty-four Puerto Ricans stop pushing their racks of dresses. They stand there watching us. Time to switch into low-gear New York street knowledge emergency procedures: Rule One — A policeman will never accidentally appear where he is needed.

I jump out of the car and begin to yell, "Help! Police! Madman!" The Puerto Ricans are looking at me. "He's been chasing us since Seventy-sixth Street," I explain.

Now they're all looking at Hugo. He lets go of the door handle. He's embarrassed. I was right. Twice.

1. The police don't show up.

2. Hugo doesn't understand he's in show biz. He's not used to lying to large audiences. He's frozen in place.

The light greens. Jack stamps down and we lurch forward. He hits the brake and we slam to a stop in front of a rack of dresses.

"Get the frock out of the way," Jack shouts at the Puerto Rican guy who pulls his rack back as we spring through the hole and into their defensive backfield. Jack stops again, leaps out, and shouts back at Hugo, "Don't worry. We'll cover for you. Just don't tell Clara."

And in he pops and he hits the gas and we begin to roll and through the rear window I can see poor Hugo, puzzled, marooned in the center of the street like the Queen Mary in Long Beach ("How could they do that? Why didn't they sink her with dignity?" my brother always says.) And Hugo is just standing there, looking at us sadly, as we fade off into the distance in his $4500 pancake pile.

"Don't worry, Hugo!" Jack shouts, laughing, as he swings past a beer truck and into the clear. "We'll mail Clara some new eyebrows from Kansas City."

Hugo, of course, can't hear him. But I know Jack's right. Hugo won't tell Clara. We'll get to Pittsburgh that night like we planned. And we'll send back the postcard to cover for him.

But somehow I can't help but feel sorry for Hugo, standing there by himself in the middle of Eleventh Avenue. I hope he didn't get run over by a live chicken truck before he made it back to the curb.

As my brother Jack would say, "On the Planet Opteema, things like this don't happen."

Chapter 3

OK. WE'RE ON THE ROAD. Crossing northern Indiana. Jack at the wheel. Me next to him, temporarily acting as Keeper-of-the-Beer. Hark in the back with the cartons of records. We've recovered from the scare we got at the last tollbooth when we saw an adult with a crew cut. We're singing jazz riffs around "Moonlight on the Wabash" and "Back Home Again in Indiana." Of course we never lived in Indiana. And we've never seen the Wabash. But we're getting into the spirit of the thing.

    I anticipate your questions, however. You've heard my voice for a few pages. Gotten to know something about me. So, I imagine you're thinking: "This guy is a reasonable enough individual. A C.P.A. A practical man. A man who spends his days over ledgers, concerning himself with such down-to-earth matters as debits and credits, assets and liabilities, percentage of bonded indebtedness and other arcane accounting concepts like "current ratio" and "Lifo" vs. "Fifo" inventory evaluation procedures.* Why is he going to California with that crazy novelist brother of his?

    I don't blame you, because I wasn't too sure myself. Jack had come up with the idea a couple months before, as we

---

*This name dropping is in the worst possible taste!
Dr. F.

drove through a light snow in New Jersey on the way home from our grandfather's burial.

His name was Isadore Farber. He was our mother's father. The rest of our grandparents were dead before we were born. Grandpa Ike had come over from Germany before World War One. He'd been a comedian. First in the Yiddish theaters, then in the hotels in the Catskills. He worked with a guy named Isador Blum who was his straight man. Maybe you heard of them. They were called, "The Two Ikes."

He was a smart man, Grandpa Ike. He invested every cent he could scrape up in apartment houses in The Bronx. At the end of World War Two, he was able to retire from show biz and just tend his buildings. He lived next door to Ike Blum and his wife Sarah, across the street from us in The Bronx. Ike Blum owned the building we lived in. Grandpa had got it for him at a bargain price and had advanced him most of the down payment.

We look like Grandpa Ike. You can see it in the old pictures of him when he was in the Yiddish theaters. And we take after him in other ways. I got his business sense. And Jack got his sense of humor.

We loved our grandfather. His jokes were corny, but once in a while he'd hit one right and crack us up. It was mostly because of him that we enlisted and went to Vietnam. He had told us, again and again, that America had saved the Jews in World War Two. He'd tried to enlist back then, but he was too old. So he traveled around and did shows for the U.S.O. He wanted us to serve in the American army.

Jack and grandpa never really got along smoothly after we came back from Nam. Grandpa was proud of Jack's purple heart. Jack wasn't. They would argue about it. Even when grandpa went to the hospital with the Big C and was shrinking away in pain, they would argue.

Our parents had moved to Florida while we were in Nam. Grandpa Ike wouldn't go. He wanted to stay on the block with Ike and Sarah Blum. He said there weren't enough jokes in Florida. We were his only relatives in New York. So, when we lived in the Village, we'd go up and see him every week.

And Jack and he would get to arguing about Vietnam. I stayed out of it. It was too bad, really. Because Jack loved the old man. Probably more than anyone else did. And he loved Jack. But after Vietnam they never really got it back together.

Anyhow, it was on the way home from grandpa's burial that Jack announced his intention to head west in the spring.

"Why California?" I asked. I was driving. Jack had been in a pretty excited state since grandpa had died. At the burial, he had worn a look of such mad grief in his eyes, I thought he might actually jump into the grave on top of the coffin.

"Are you kidding? California is America squared. One last 3000-mile chance for people who couldn't make it on their first trip to the new world."

"But we *are* making it in the new world. We're successful. I'm an accountant. You're a novelist . . ."

"It's not enough for me, Jerr. Maybe it's enough for you, but it isn't enough for me. I'm going west. Anything's possible in California."

Well, he wasn't in a very stable place. And he didn't seem to improve as the weeks passed. So I decided to go with him. I mean, he *was* my brother.

But I can't completely kid myself and put it all on Jack. I guess I wanted something too. I couldn't say what it was . . . Something I wasn't getting out of my life. It wasn't enough for me either.

So here we were, in April, in Hugo's car, sipping our Iron City beer and heading west. (We always support the local breweries. My brother doesn't want them to die out.)

"Oh, man, we're gonna have such a great time," Jack said. "Anything's possible in California. I've got this idea for having two lamps over my bed. I'm gonna find me a woman who can make love and read at the same time. We can make it during the adjectives . . . Hey, want to stop at South Bend? See Notre Dame? Walk around the campus? Check out the stadium?"

He's got me there. I love stadiums. Especially old baseball parks. You see, my brother and I grew up near Yankee Stadium. We used to go there all the time. And to the old Polo Grounds, too. We'd walk across the old walking bridge from The Bronx to Manhattan. The one with the two-car subway shuttle on it. They tore down the Polo Grounds to build a housing project. They even tore down the old walking bridge.

We loved to go out to the ballpark. We'd go early and pay our sixty cents and sit out in the sunshine in the bleachers and read Russian novels until the game started. I finished the last couple chapters of *The Brothers Karamazov* at the Polo Grounds one day before a Giant-Dodger game. What a great day that was. First all those kids shouting, "Hooray for Karamazov!" to Alyosha, and then Carl Furillo throwing the ball at Leo Durocher after Sal the Barber Maglie gave him too close a shave at the plate.

Life was full then. At the ballpark. When I could forget about my "real" life. Outside.

Sometimes I would go by myself. You'd be surprised how alone you can feel, sitting in an old ballpark. Even with ten thousand people around. If you didn't grow up in the country with trees and all, it's the only place you could go to think about things.

"Root, root for old Notre Dame," Jack is singing as he pulls out to pass a big Safeway truck, "You take the Notre and I'll take the Dame."

We smile together. Another Junior High School 82 Special.

"Jack, you remember that time we went to Griffith Stadium in Washington?"

"Sure do. Four hundred six feet down the left field line. It took a Paul Bunyan to hit one out of there . . . You think it's still there?"

"Nah . . . I imagine they tore it down when they built that new RFK Stadium."

"I don't like these new suburban stadiums."

"Me neither," I said.

"They all look alike."

"Anyone can build a big bowl in the middle of a field."

"Yeah, but you give a guy a little odd-shaped lot in the center of a city and you tell him to build a ballpark on it . . . man, that's *architecture!*"

Hark reached his head over the seat and nuzzled my ear with his wet nose. I patted him on his head. Jack said, "You know what I would've liked to have done? Taken a trip across country going from ballpark to ballpark. Then we could've *seen* the places we used to hear about on the radio when the teams were on the road."

"We could've taken a quick trip to Boston to look at the short left field wall in Fenway Park."

"No, I mean all of them, Jerr. Shibe Park in Philly, and Forbes Field in Pittsburgh, and Crosley Field in Cincinnati . . ."

"They're all gone now."

"I know . . . Damn it, any other country would've preserved them. It isn't right. They were our Gothic cathedrals."

We approached South Bend from the north. I sat quietly.

"Why don't we go through Chicago, Jerr? If the Cubs are in town, we can take in a game at Wrigley Field."

"I don't know . . . We're already way off the route . . . And we're supposed to go through St. Louis."

"The St. Louis Browns aren't there anymore, Jerr. They're the Baltimore Orioles now . . . It might depress me."

"No . . . It'll be OK."

"And they tore down Sportsman's Park."

"I want to see the arch. They have these little cars that go up it so the people put up the money to build it. They think it's a ride. But it's really art."

"Well, OK. How about if we go there after Chicago. First we can check out the vines on the outfield wall at Wrigley Field. And remember, they never even put up lights there, Jerr. They still play all their games during the day. Think of it . . ."

I smiled. Good old Jack. He knew I couldn't resist seeing a ballpark with vines on the outfield fences.

"And we can check out the art museum," I said.

"Sure. And the science museum, too."

"And we'll go hear some music on the South Side."

"You know it. Right after we check out the home of the Fighting Irish we head for the Windy City." He turned to his left and shouted out his window, "HOG BUTCHER TO A NATION! LOOK OUT GENE AMMONS! LOOK OUT NELSON ALGREN! LOOK OUT LOUIS SULLIVAN! LOOK OUT ANDY PAFCO! HERE WE COME!

"*Jack!*"

He slammed down on the brakes. We'd almost run up the back of the car in front of us as he shouted.

He laughed. "Don't worry about Clara and her insurance. Everything'll be OK. With you riding shotgun we'll never crash." He turned to me. "OK?"

"OK."

"That's more like it. New Beginnings. That's the message. New beginnings. New York was OK. But it's too tight. The capital of Pesseema. The ultimate twentieth century city . . ."

"But this *is* the twentieth century."

"Only on the calendar, Jerr. Only on the calendar. In California we'll be able to let go."

"Maybe so . . ."

"No 'maybe' about it . . . After California the only place left to go is Vietnam and you saw where that one got us."

"Well, I hope we can swing it."

"We will, Jerr. It's Opteema for us from now on."

Hark reached over the seat and licked Jack's ear, making him laugh. "That's where we're going to , my man. The Planet Opteema." He turned and began to shout out his window again at the moving Indiana countryside, "GOODBYE SMOG-HOBBLED METROPOLIS! WITH YOUR CRIME AND YOUR STREETS. GOODBYE MOTHER OF THE TRAGIC VIEW."

"Jack, watch the road."

"HELLO GOLDEN WEST! GOODBYE PESSIMISTIC CIVILIZATION. HELLO BEACH BOYS. GET YOUR WOODIES AND YOUR WAHEENIES. OPTEEMA HERE WE COME!"

"I hope so," I said to myself, quietly. But Jack probably wouldn't have heard me anyway. He was steering with his left hand, patting Hark's big head (resting on his shoulder) with his right, and singing:

> Take back your New York joys
> I'm bound for Illi-noise
> Just-as-fast-as-I-can

And it sounded so good I couldn't help but join in.

Chapter 4

WHEN YOU'RE IN AN ELEVATOR by yourself do you ever tap-dance?

But I'm getting ahead of myself. Since I'm on the subject of South Bend, I guess I should describe the next stage of my brother's matzo fetish.

It happened in a hamburger joint on the north side of town. We stopped there after we toured the campus of Notre Dame. I don't remember the name of the place. It was right near a big dry cleaners and it had a parking lot in front. We left our car there and walked into the hamburger joint. Jack and Hark and me.

I wasn't sure taking Hark into a hamburger joint in Indiana was such a good idea. In fact, I wasn't sure that going to look at the home of the "Fighting Irish" was such a good idea either. Especially when I noticed that my brother was always managing to walk within the sight of at least one priest where it was "safe." I think the Fighting Irish vibes of Notre Dame re-vibrated some old street chord in my brother's mind.

When we left the relative security of our station wagon for the greasy spoon, he made sure Hark was right beside him. He even sat Hark at a seat at our table. The waitress, a fortyish woman with a heavyset body and bleached blond hair, didn't notice our entrance because she was walking into the kitchen as we came in.

But I guess even the presence of Hark beside him wasn't enough for Jack.

"I don't like the looks of this," he said, scanning the other customers.

There were ten men, three women, and four kids.

"Ten against two," Jack said.

"This is Indiana. They won't bother us. They're *Americans.*"

But before I could stop him, he leaps up out of his seat and begins to dance a kind of jig around the place, singing, "Shake hands with your uncle Mike, me boy. And here's your sister Kate . . . " Well, the people looked at him like he was nuts but he kept it up, "And there's the girl you used to swing, down by the garden gate . . . ," moving from table to table, dancing with back straight, head held high, singing at the top of his voice and looking at each group of people as if he expected them to jump up and join him. I don't have to tell you this caused quite a commotion. One middle-aged couple got the hell out of there even before they ordered their food. When no one joined Jack, he danced back to our table. ("You're as welcome as the flowers in May, To dear old Donegal.") He didn't notice the waitress steaming up behind him, looking as moral and legal as a Lincoln Continental.

"We're safe," Jack said, relaxing into his seat next to Hark. "If there were any Irish here, they would have joined in."

"Hey, what's with your friend?" the waitress says to me. She does a double take when she sees we're twins, and then a triple (or even a home run) take when she sees huge Hark sitting nonchalantly at the table. "And what's *this?* You can't bring a dog into a restaurant! What's with you guys?"

Well, as you can imagine, this was very embarrassing to me. I mean, granted, I had quit my job when we left New York, but I had not quit my profession as well. You just don't stop being a C.P.A. when you cross a state line, let me tell you. I mean, you can understand. Suppose one of my clients had seen me there, sitting at a table in an Indiana hamburger stand with a dancing madman and a giant dog.

But just as I was about to apologize and take Hark back to the car, Jack looks up at her and he says, bluntly, "Madam! This is not a dog. This is my son."

"Jack . . . "

But the peroxide interrupts me. Angry now. "Look. You just get that mutt out of here!"

Well, here she got *my* dander up. I mean you can say what you want to about me, but that's no reason to call my dog a mutt. So I ups and says, "Madam, that dog may not be this gentleman's son, but he is an innocent party to this human dispute and there is absolutely no reason to cast aspersions on the legitimacy of his birth."

"All right! Whatever! Just get him the hell out of here!"

Jack turns to me. "Gerald, did you hear that? That fiery tone. The ardent yearning in the voice. The forceful emphasis in the elocution. And the power of that single pause between 'All right' and 'Whatever.' That's exactly what opera has been missing since Louise Homer died. Did you *hear* that pause?"

Jack rises and exclaims, in a deep theatrical tone, to the people at the other tables who are all watching us now:

"One soft first pause and last.

One, — then the old rage of rapture's fieriest rain

Storms all the music-maddened night again."

Three guys drinking beer at a table in the corner begin to applaud. Several other people join in. Jack smiles, makes a sweeping formal bow, and announces, "Swinburne, gentlemen. Swinburne."

Then, sitting back down, he says, "Madam, my brother and I are not tourists although we often masquerade as such in our tours of the countryside. Actually, I am Mr. Rudolph Bing, director of the Metropolitan Opera Company of New York, and my brother here is Mr. . . . er . . . Crosby Bing, my accountant and financial advisor. I think I can speak for both of us when I offer you a con . . . "

"I'll Bing you, buddy!"

It's a new voice. I look up. We're a quartet now. The bass-baritone has arrived. It's the cook. And he's big. And he's got a butcher knife in his hand.

My brother "Rudolph" spots him and immediately goes into Bronx S.O.P. rules 2A and 2B:

2A. Always yield to superior force. Let the Japanese worry about saving face; in The Bronx you just worry about saving your ass.

2B. *Never*, repeat, *never* fight with anyone who is armed, regardless of any differentials in height, weight, sex, age, general physique, or country of national origin.

Jack is silent.

"Well, look, let's be reasonable," I say.

"Get that Great Dane out of here!" the cook says.

"Certainly, sir," I say, rising from my seat. "Jack, let's comply with the armed gentleman's wish."

But Jack says, "Sir, that dog is not a Great Dane. He is a Great Danish."

The cook's face reddens and he steps toward Jack. Hark gives him a low-throated growl that freezes him in his tracks. Jack smiles and says, "But nevertheless we will comply with your reasonable demands. Hark. Go outside."

Jack points to the door. Hark walks slowly away from us, watching the cook over his shoulder as he leaves. He opens the glass door with his nose and sits down right outside, his eyes still fixed on the cook. When things quiet down, the cook thaws and walks back into his kitchen, shaking his head and muttering to himself.

"OK, what'll you guys have?" the waitress says.

"I'll have a Knute Rockne Burger," I say.

"And to drink?"

"Coffee."

"And you?"

"I'll have a Matzo Burger," Jack says.

She begins to write. Then, "*What?*"

"A Matzo Burger."

She looks to me.

"Jack . . ."

"I want a Matzo Burger."

"What the hell is this 'Mazza Burger?'" she says to me.

I'm about to explain that a matzo is a kind of cracker, unleavened bread the Jewish people had to eat on the trek out of Egypt, when Jack says, "A Matzo Burger is a specialty of the Jewish people. When we had to leave Egypt there was no yeast in the desert. So at every MacDonald's we stopped at, we had to eat our hamburgers on unleavened buns."

"What?"

"That was tough times," Jack says. "The pharaoh had just

tried to wipe us out by giving the order to kill the oldest male child of every delicatessen owner in Egypt. Fortunately for us, Charlton Heston showed up just in time to part the sea and get us the hell out of there."

"That's true," I say. "No one could make up something like that."

"Well, whatever," she says. "We don't have no Mazza Burger. We got a Gipper Burger. We got a Four Horseman Special with fries. We got Veal Parseghian. But we don't have no Mazza Burger. So make up your mind before I get Mike back out here with a cleaver."

"You have a Watermelon Burger?" Jack says. "To honor all the great Black guys who played basketball here?"

"Mike!" She turns toward the kitchen. I leap up and cut her off at the pass. Fortunately Mike and his butcher knife didn't hear her.

"Look, just give him a Cardinal Spellman Fish Fry and a Pope Leo XIII shake."

"Well, that's a little more like it." She scribbles on her pad. "What's with that guy anyway?"

"He's only kidding around."

"Well, that's some kind of kidding!"

"He hasn't been the same since he got back from Vietnam."

"*He's* a veteran?"

"Oh, yeah. Purple heart and everything. He got shot in the foot . . ."

"A short VC sniper got me from the side with a low shot," Jack says. "Took off all ten of my toes."

She looks toward me.

"It's true," I say. "I swear it."

"When they finally found all my toes, they shipped them back to the States in a Thom McAn shoe box with a tiny American flag draped around it."

"It was really sad."

"Are you kidding me? What do you think I am?" she says.

"A good sport," I smile.

She walks into the kitchen. I sit back down with Jack at the table. Never realizing at the time that what appeared to be the subject of a single matzo joke would become the object of a fetish a month after we got to California.

22

Chapter 5

I PROMISED MYSELF I'D EXPLAIN this Opteema-Pesseema business before we got to the Rocky Mountains so I better do it now. It comes from my brother's novel, *The Majority Hallucination* (which is his name for "reality"). The book is narrated by a man who claims to be from a wonderful planet called Opteema. But somehow he's gotten stuck on a planet he calls Pesseema where people have come to believe in a philosophy that the narrator sums up as, "The deeper you go, the darker it gets."

At first he's deeply troubled at finding himself in such a strange, gloomy place. But then, in true Opteeman fashion, he comes up with the idea that maybe he was sent to Pesseema to enlighten the people, to show them that reality is only a shared hallucination of the majority of the people at a particular time and place—a kind of "novel" in which they've come to live—and that they've gotten themselves into a bad novel that doesn't make them happy. So he travels around Pesseema to spread the word. To give people a better hallucination in which to live.

He meets all these interesting people and when he gets to know them he tells them where he's from and he explains, "The deeper you go, the darker it gets. But only for a little while. If you dig deep enough, you come out in India. And if you go even further, you wind up in the sky."

Well, he means well, and some of the people are very nice to him, but, to his surprise, the inhabitants of Pesseema turn out to have what he calls, "A patriotism toward tragedy." When he tries to challenge this, they decide to help him by putting him in a hospital in order to bring him "out of the clouds and down to Pesseema."

In the hospital he begins to get depressed again, so he invents a novel to live in that has him beginning his work again with the psychiatrist they send in each day to help him. He figures he was meant to start by convincing one intelligent man and that the hour a day with the shrink will give him the perfect opportunity to do this. So he begins again, calmly explaining to the doctor that the world is sad only because we imagine it that way, and that the way to change the world is to change the way we imagine it. He says the Pesseemans are living in a novel in which death is the worst thing that can happen. But that in fact there's no more reason to think of death as bad than as good. The question is completely open. So it's best to see death, and life, in a way that makes you happy in the present. And this better novel is the Planet Opteema. He claims it is this pessimistic view of death that leads to a futile grasping at life and possessions, and ultimately, to war.

Of course, he fails again. And he remains locked up in the mental hospital, and we can guess he'll never get out of there because the book ends with a "verbatim transcript" of an hour session with him and the shrink after two years of daily treatment, and we see he will no longer say anything serious, but responds to everything the shrink says with old one-liner jokes.

I liked that last chapter the best. It was bitter, and it was really sad, but it was also funny because my brother included every joke he could remember from our days in The Bronx. So even though I felt really sorry for the guy, locked up forever in a crazy house, I couldn't stop laughing at his jokes.

Maybe you read it. It came out a year later in paperback as part of a series they called, "Science Fiction and Fantasy Novels."

My brother wasn't happy about this label. He says all science is just another fiction. And "reality" is just one possible fantasy.

I can see what he's getting at. But I don't agree. I'm no philosopher, but I am a damn good accountant, and I know that both sides of the balance sheet have got to match. I don't care what planet you live on, you can't get something for nothing. If you get a life, there's an outstanding claim against it that someday's gonna come due. So I say that whether you claim to live on Opteema or not, you better not get too comfortable in your room here, because, underneath, some part of you knows that you're just a guest in the Earth Hotel, and you know someday the management's gonna ask you to check out.

My brother was really disappointed when his book failed to change the world. He'd always been a bit of a manic-depressive, but after he served in Vietnam his mood swings became more severe, from extravagant plans and hopes to quick depression at the first sign of failure. And the fights with grandpa didn't help him any either.

Anyhow, we got out of South Bend alive, and we made it to Wrigley Field and saw the famous outfield wall with the vines on it. And that night we went to South Chicago, over by Cottage Grove and South Sixty-third, to hear some jazz.

Then we continued on, through Illinois and across the Mississippi into Iowa. I'll say this about my brother: he may be nuts (I mean not exactly down to Earth) but he's sure fun to travel with. If I was by myself I think I would have just zipped across on Clara's route and stayed insured. I like the scenery too, but that's probably what I would've done. The "wide open spaces" make me nervous. You're out there all by yourself and there's no cops around.

And in the Rockies at night I kept thinking we might meet a bear. I wasn't really *afraid* of meeting a bear, but I never learned the *etiquette* of it, if you know what I mean.

Anyhow, traveling with Jack transformed everything into an event. Every place we came to got him excited. First we were "on the road" (in *New Jersey*, goddamnit!). Then we came to the "Old Northwest Territory" (it looked like Ohio to me). Then we were heading for the "Great American West." I'll tell you the truth, for me the Great American West began with that guy with the crew cut in the tollbooth in Ohio. When I see an adult with a crew cut I get the heebie-jeebies. Maybe it's racial memory or something, but they all look like their names are Fritz or Hans.

I don't know about you, but the only kaiser I ever liked

was Kaiser-Frazer. (Remember that car? A Frazer? Wouldn't it be great to have one now? You get a date for the evening with this terrific lady and you pull up in a 1947 Frazer, and she says, "That's a quaint automobile," and you say, nonchalantly, "Oh, it's nothing. It's just my Frazer.")

Anyhow, my brother wasn't a believer in the straightest line between two points. We had to make all these detours. Like we had to go to Peoria, Illinois, to see Bradley University because they had played City College in the N.I.T. finals about twenty years ago. We'd gone to the game. And we had rooted for Bradley. They seemed so *American* to us.

And then we had to drive through downtown Rock Island, Illinois, at midnight when everything was closed anyhow, and I said, "Jack, why did we have to do this?" and he said, sitting there next to me, wide awake, digging everything, "Are you kidding? This is *Rock Island*," and I said, "Oh, Rock Island," and he smiled at me, his face lit with joy in the dark car, and I didn't have the heart to tell him I didn't have the vaguest idea of what he was talking about.

And then, as we were crossing the Mississippi, well, as the country folks say, "He like to went crazy." Shouting about "Life on the Mississippi" and Huck Finn and Mike Fink and singing "Old Man River" and God knows what else. I'll tell you the truth, the Mississippi was kind of a disappointment to me. Maybe I expected too much, but it really just seemed like a big muddy river. But as for my brother Jack, well, he was carrying on so as we drove across the bridge, I swear I don't think he saw the real river at all.

But he had been just as wild in Pittsburgh, where we had to get off the Pennsylvania Turnpike and drive through all the downtown traffic to the point where the two rivers meet, and Jack got out and started ranting about, "The confluence of the great Allegheny and the mighty Monongahela to form the vast Ohio." Well, he didn't notice, but everyone was looking at us and I was embarrassed as hell.

But the next day, driving through Indiana, when he gave me a history of the different kinds of flat boats that went down the Ohio, and the canals of the midwest that they built before they built the railroads, and when he told me about the steamboat races on the Mississippi and how they would cause the boilers to blow up in these big explosions that killed hundreds of people, and how, even so, when two boats would come up alongside each other all the passengers would egg the captains on to race, and they *would* race, and more boats would get blown up, and more people would get killed, well, I'll admit it, when he would talk like that it sure made the trip a hell of a lot more interesting than just driving across country by yourself and staying on the route.

My brother Jack is a terrific talker—one of the best—and I'm not just prejudiced because he's my brother. I only wish he hadn't stopped writing, so you could hear him for yourself.

Chapter 6

I'M TRYING TO KEEP this book short because paper's expensive, but I seem to keep following my brother on all these detours he makes. At one point, we had to go 200 miles out of our way to go across the border into New Mexico and I said, "What's the point, Jack?" and he said, "It's another state, man! Another state." But I couldn't see the difference, really.

When we got to the Painted Desert, Jack went up to the ranger station and asked them if the landlord painted it every three years like he was required to by law, and the rangers looked at him as if he was nuts and I was embarrassed as hell again and glad to get out of there.

Finally, we arrived, late in the afternoon, at the Grand Canyon. And, as I guess you could predict by now, Jack went wild and I was a little disappointed. I mean, it was OK, but to me, at least at first, it was too much like all the pictures on the Ferde Grofé *Grand Canyon Suite* record albums. I felt like I had been there before.

We parked our station wagon, threw a stick to Hark for a while to give him some exercise, and then walked toward the rim of the canyon. A lizard startled me. It crept out from under a rock, jerked a look up at us, and then scurried away.

"What's the matter?"

"The lizard. It's the first one I've ever seen."

"Wait till you see a zucchini. Then you'll have seen everything."

We walked up to the edge of the down-drop. The sun was beginning to set.

"I've been dreaming about this for years," Jack said.

But I couldn't concentrate on the view. I was on the watch for lizards.

"Don't worry about it," Jack said.

"I don't know. These things might come in pairs."

"They're OK. They eat bugs and stuff. They're important to the ecology."

"Oh, yeah, well if they're so terrific, why don't they have them in New York? The greatest city in the world and you think, if lizards are so terrific, they're not going to have lizards there? Come off it."

Then I noticed a strange pair of eyes looking at me from over on the left. It turned out to be a representative of another species I had never encountered before. *Tourista Okeeana.* This one was from Muskogee. He was about sixty-five years old, wearing a long, loose, red sport jacket and blue pleated pants. He walked up to us and began to talk in a loud voice about a man named Lucas Benson.

"Please, sir," Jack said, "you're interrupting the sunset."

He laughed. He thought Jack was kidding. He turned to me. "Lucas Benson's nephew! Well I'll be darned. I didn't recall you had yourself a twin brother." He reached out to shake hands. "Lem Tucker from Muskogee. I'm sure right pleased to meet you again."

Before I could reply, Jack said, sharply, "Sir, please, you are in the wrong part of the park. The set for the Grapes of Wrath is about a mile south of here. In fact, I think I just saw Henry Fonda walking in that direction. Perhaps if you pile your family and all your possessions into the back of your old pick-up you'll still be able to catch up with him."

Jack turned away and attempted, once again, to watch the sunset.

"I'll be dog tied and hog varnished," Lem said to me, ignoring Jack. "Think of it! Running into Lucas Benson's nephew here at the Grand Canyon. Sarah!" he shouted to his wife, who was sitting in their station wagon. "Sarah! Looka here! Lucas Benson's nephew."

Sarah approached. Plump and bouncy. Wearing a red-checkered pant suit. She walked up to me, took my chin in her hands like a painter, and turned my face to the light so she could examine it in profile.

"Yep," she said, still holding my chin in her heavy hand, "he favors Lucas, all right."

"Did you say her name was Sarah?" Jack asked Lem as he watched her studying the lines and shadows of my face.

"That's right, sonny."

"That's funny. If you hadn't told me her name, I would have sworn she was Georgia O'Keeffe."

Sarah finally released my chin from her paw. Both *Tourista Okeeanas* kept smiling. "Lucas Benson!" the male exclaimed once again. "In the big depression, Lucas Benson held back on foreclosing my mortgage for three years. Three years! Any nephew of Lucas Benson's is a nephew of mine."

"Look, *uncle*," Jack said, "I think you'd better be running along. I hear President Andy Jackson's moving the Cherokees out to Oklahoma from Georgia. They'll be attacking your home any day now. You better go stock up on flints and provisions."

"I'll be darned," the male said, looking at my face again. "What ever happened to your Aunt Ella?"

"What ever happened to Pee Wee Marquette?" Jack snapped at him.

"Pee Wee Marquette?" Uncle Lem said, finally acknowledging him. "Who's this Pee Wee Marquette?"

"The colored midget who used to introduce the acts at Birdland," Jack said, turning back to the sunset.

"Well, you just stop by and stay with us anytime," Uncle Lem said to me, once again ignoring Jack.

"He took tickets at the door, too," Jack said.

"Who?" Aunt Sarah said.

"*Pee Wee Marquette*, damn it!" Jack said.

"Well, I don't know any Pee Wee . . . ," Uncle Lem said.

"Please, sir," Jack said, "I'm trying to peruse the sunset in peace."

" . . . but I know about Lucas Benson . . . "

"What is he? Some kind of Red?" Jack said.

"Some kinda Red? Hell no. He was a good American."

"Oh, good," Jack said. "For a minute there I thought he might be a follower of the great dry-witted leader of the Chinese Revolution, Chairman Matzo Tongue."

Uncle Lem looked puzzled for a second. Then he and Aunt Sarah turned to leave, once again inviting us Bensons to stay with them when we got to Muskogee. We didn't tell them we were going in the other direction.

Even after they were gone, Jack continued to be upset. There were still other tourists around. He wanted to be able to "peruse the sunset in peace." So he attempted to drive them off. Using two separate tactics.

First, he did a series of Martha and the Vandellas impersonations. His "Heat Wave" alone succeeded in ridding us of almost half of them.

Then, as the sun dilated on the horizon, and the air chilled quickly, he took a blanket from the car, put it over his head, and began to do a wild Indian dance (Hark doing his playful Great Dane dance beside him) on the edge of the rim, dancing back and forth toward the tourists in either direction, singing a kind of rhythmic, menacing, "*Hey* ya, *Hey* ya, *Hey* ya, *Hey* ya," like Jay Silverheels (Tonto) did when he came to visit the assembly at our elementary school in The Bronx—P.S. 11. (Or at least it seems to me now that he sang when he visited us.) Anyway, Jack hooted and bounced about in a way that seemed to threaten the tourists who hadn't been driven away by his Martha and the Vandellas impersonation.

So we got to "peruse the sunset in peace." And, speaking as an accountant, I'll have to admit that, given the value added by the asset of the sunset, it really was more profitable to see the canyon in person than on the cover of a Ferde Grofé record. The sun seemed to fry the parched sky into an orange tint that gently, and surprisingly, died into mauve.

It was as good as any light show I ever saw at the old Fillmore East on Second Avenue.

Chapter

7

THE MOJAVE DESERT is the Grand Canyon in spades. I couldn't see the point of it. It was like Jones Beach without the ocean.

Jack liked the spring flowers that punctuated the blank pages of the desert. He stopped the car to take a closer look. Hark bounded out and did his floppy stretch-yawn dance. I wouldn't go out with them.

"What's the matter with you?" Jack said, coming around to the outside of my open window. "The desert is beautiful."

"Not to me."

"Come on out."

"I'm afraid."

"There's no rattlers around here."

"I'm afraid of the cactus."

Hark ran up to Jack and pushed against him playfully with his paws.

"We'll take Hark with us."

"He grew up in Greenwich Village. What does he know from cactus?"

"Are you crazy, man? This is great! Come on!"

"Look, if I want to see the desert, I can go to an Antonioni movie."

"That costs three bucks."

"It's worth it."

"Oh, man," he said, turning toward the flowers. "Come on, Hark."

"Oh, no. Hark stays here with me."

"Are you kidding? There may be snakes out there."

"Before, you said there weren't any."

"That was before."

So Jack and Hark went off to see the desert spring flowers. Although, to tell you the truth, I don't think I was really afraid. It was more a role I'd gotten into playing because it gave me the chance to be funny.

Still, if I want the feel of the desert, I can stay home and read Paul Bowles. We accountants are a lot smarter than some literary guys think we are. We read too, damn it. Accounting is a lot more sophisticated than a lot of people think. You try to figure out what it costs General Motors to make a Chevrolet and you'll see. I mean, when Connie Lou McKinsley at GM headquarters calls her mother in Baton Rouge on the company phone, how much of that three bucks goes toward the cost of a single Chevy? And how much toward the cost of making a Cadillac? You see what I mean? It's not so simple.

But where was I? Oh, yeah, the desert. I lost my taste for the desert when I was in the army. In South Texas rattler country. They were training me and Jack and our friend Wheeler to fly med-evac helicopters over the jungle, so they figured one of the most important things we'd have to learn would be what to do if we got lost, alone, in the desert, at night.

So they took us, and our fellow trainees, out into the desert, down near the Mexican border somewhere, and they shot a few five-foot long rattlers that afternoon (just to convince us to be careful, if you know what I mean) and then, at midnight, they dropped each of us off, alone, seven miles from camp, armed with a compass and a snake bite kit, and they said, "See you back at camp in the morning."

Well, I'll admit it, nothing in my Bronx street training had prepared me for this. And the god-damned armadillos scurrying about didn't help much either. I couldn't tell the difference between them and rattlers in the dark, because in The Bronx, see (and I know this may be hard to believe) we didn't *have* any god-damned armadillos. (In fact, we wouldn't have them if you paid us. The damn things are too *dumb* to live in The Bronx.)

Anyway, I got enough of the desert that night to last me for quite a while. But I did get to learn one valuable lesson. See, growing up in The Bronx, I never had much contact with Protestants. In fact, we only had one Protestant guy in our neighborhood. A Scotch guy. His name was Jimmy. We used to call him "The Protestant."

Well, that night on the desert in Texas, I got to know what a White Protestant American is. You see, I didn't tell you that dropping us out in the middle of Rattlesnakeville wasn't enough for the geniuses in the army. They had to make it "realistic." So they had these choppers flying overhead with searchlights, trying to catch us. And when they'd spot one of us, they'd come down real low and throw bags of flour at him. And if he got hit by the flour, he had to walk all the way back across the damn desert to where they first dropped him off, and start again.

They got me when I was about halfway home—after three miles of torture. Well, I don't think I have to tell you I wasn't going across any three miles of rattler-hotel to start again. So I just ran like a son-of-a-bitch in the other direction and some guy in the chopper started yelling down at me through a loudspeaker, "Hey, there! We got you. Go back to the beginning."

"Fuck you, General," I shouted, and I ran like hell and hid under some kind of stunted tree until the assholes got tired of flying around looking for me and took off and I could finally come out and dust the flour off my fatigues and continue on my merry way home.

But, you see, while I was out there, stumbling around from stunted tree to stunted tree, I saw other guys from my platoon get hit by sacks of flour. American guys. And that's when I found out what a White Protestant American is. You take a White Protestant American and you drop him in the middle of rattlesnake country at night, unarmed, and you put guys in helicopters above him, chasing him around and dropping stuff on him, and you have some guy from the government tell him it's a game, and if he gets flour on his shirt he's got to go back to the beginning and start again, and you let him make it for six miles alive, and then you hit him with some flour and that son-of-a-bitch is going to go back over the same six miles to the beginning and start again.

This is true. I actually saw it happen. Again and again. I swear, I couldn't believe it. I'd never seen anything like that in my life before. That would be like taking a Bronx guy and dropping him off at night over past Theodore Roosevelt High School on East Fordham Road and telling him he's got to make it back to the West Bronx alive, alone and unarmed, through Fordham Baldie territory.

That's right. The Fordham Baldies. The most terrifying gang in East Bronx history. No one in the West Bronx even knew if they really existed. And no one was willing to find out. They were *more* terrifying because we'd never seen them. We didn't even know if they had hair or not. They were mythological, goddamnit! *Mythological!* That's how terrifying they were.

Well, you take a Bronx guy and drop him off there, and you let him make it back alive and unscarred to the West Bronx, and then, just when he's getting to The Grand Concourse, you hit him with some fucking *flour* and you say, "We got you. Start again, Mario," and you see what he does to you. You just try it and see.

That's why I couldn't understand a White Protestant American if I lived a million years.

Chapter 8

OK, I ADMIT IT, I went out there to look at the spring flowers. I couldn't resist. I was fascinated by the desert colors.

The distinctions between color on the desert were so fine it was like when you're trying to raise money for a corporation and you have to decide whether to float common stock, or maybe preferred, or else borrow the money long term by issuing corporate bonds at 8¾% (or maybe at 9% which is more expensive but more attractive to the buyer). You have to look long and hard to see the subtle distinctions. Well, that's what the desert reminded me of.

Anyhow, we're out there, in the middle of the Mojave, which is as close to the middle of Nowhere as you're going to get here on our beloved Planet Pesseema (as Jack would say), when suddenly Jack lights up—"Do you realize we're in *California*? Do you *realize* it? We made it."

Well, it looked just like your average desert to me, but Jack begins to run around in these big circles with Hark flop-dancing after him and Jack shouts, "Surf's up! Get your woodies! Get your waheenies! Hang ten!" And he starts singing old Beach Boy hits in the middle of the goddamn Mojave desert.

Well, I was glad at least Hark was enjoying it. I was kind of embarrassed, myself. I kept looking around to see if anyone was watching.

But after a while, Jack began to reach me. Especially when he started to tap-dance. You see, we had this tap-dancing act worked out when we were teenagers. Of course, we rarely did it in public. Only, say, for our basketball team, the Highbridge Pioneers, on the platform of a lonely, night el-station, after a big victory against the 183rd Street Navajos or some tough team like that. (Never in front of girls!)

If you remember, there used to be this act on TV called the Four Step Brothers. Each would step forward to take a solo while the other three brothers would stamp their feet, and point toward him, and yell, "Hey! Hey! Hey! Hey!" and the guy in front would do all these impossible steps. Well, Jack and I worked up an act we called "The Two Schlep Brothers." First, we would tap-dance like mad, not together or anything, just like mad, but we would pretend we thought we were dancing in unison. Then I would step back and go, "Hey! Hey! Hey!" and point toward Jack who would try all these impossible steps, but each time he would mess up and take this terrific fall right on his back, and he'd get up and try another one, and whammo! right down again, and all the time I would be standing behind him, smiling like crazy, making believe I didn't see a thing going wrong, shouting, "Hey! Hey! Hey!" and looking proudly toward the audience like I thought my brother was the greatest dancer in the world.

Then Jack would step back and I would begin to take the falls. We would end with that step that tap-dancing acts always end with, where you lean forward together, facing the audience, and you begin to run stiff-legged in place, as if you were running on ice, and you swing your arms, stiffly, out toward the audience, as if you were bowling balls at them with each hand, right, left, right, left, and everyone applauds like mad, not because it's so hard to do, but because they've all seen acts like this before and they know it's the finale, and you did your part and danced like crazy, and now it's their turn to do their part and applaud like mad.

Well, my brother began to dance, right there in the middle of the Mojave, singing, "California, here I come, right back where I started from," under the one-hundred degree, hot afternoon sun, and Hark began to jump up and down with him, and when Jack turned to me I'll be damned if I didn't start to stamp my foot and point at him and go, "Hey! Hey! Hey!" while he did his falls.

And then, I have to admit it, when he finished, and stepped back, and pointed at me, and began *his*, "Hey! Hey! Hey!" I began to do mine.

What the hell.

Anyhow, our mood got higher and higher as we approached San Francisco. In fact, we almost peaked a little early. In Fresno. We got stopped by the police there when Jack got out of the car on a downtown street corner and began to do Frankie Laine imitations for the crowd. "Jezebel" and "Rose, Rose, I Love You" and all the corny old songs we used to listen to before we found out about WLIB in Harlem, and Alan Freed's rhythm and blues on WINS, and Symphony Sid's all night jazz on WEVD (the station named after Eugene V. Debs).

Well, someone in Fresno panicked and called the cops, and they were pretty close to giving us a motel room in the slammer until I began to talk accounting to them, and they realized I was OK. So they agreed to let me take my brother away if he would promise not to do any more Frankie Laine imitations in the downtown area. Of course, as we were leaving the station, Jack couldn't leave well enough alone and he almost blew it by asking them if he could at least do one Teresa Brewer at a shopping center.

Believe me, it took a lot of fast talking on my part to get us out of that one.

Chapter 9

SAN FRANCISCO is the kind of city where they put nets on the baskets in the schoolyards and no one steals them. We crossed into the city over the Oakland Bay Bridge, singing harmony on the Mamas and the Papas' old tune, "California Dreamin'."

It was a crisp, clear afternoon with wisps of fog floating low over the city from the west. We were to drop off the station wagon and be met by our friend Wheeler Finkelstein and his wife Becky. We would only stay briefly in the city. We were through with cities. My brother Jack said they were the heart of Pesseema. And we wanted to get out of Pesseema. And to get Pesseema out of ourselves. "To tear it out by the roots if necessary. The negative conditioning is deeper than we can imagine. We need new beginnings. Freedom or death." (At least that's what my brother Jack said.)

We stopped at You-Go's office to drop off our station wagon, leaving our records locked in it in their basement parking lot. The office was on Market Street which, if you don't know San Francisco, is a pretty seedy place. Cheap double-feature movie houses, porn flicks, and stores that sell subtle clothes like pink sport jackets and string ties that look like saxophone holders without their saxophones.

Three thousand miles and we were back in Times Square. But with a difference. There was a kind of western innocence about the place. The crazy violent vibes weren't as strong as on Forty-second Street. It seemed like a bunch of bums from the country trying to be big time but they just weren't cracked, scared, hard, or berserk enough to really pull it off.

"You see Wheeler around, Jack?"

"No."

I looked at my watch. "We've got a half hour to kill."

"Let's walk up this street a bit."

"I want to get some socks."

We walked up Market Street, Hark heeling on Jack's left.

"I'm anxious to meet Wheeler's new wife," I said.

"All I know about her is her name is Becky." We passed a movie theater showing *Junior High Madam*. "Did he tell you she works at the synagogue or something?"

"I think he said she helps out the social director."

"So Wheeler married a nice Jewish girl after all."

We came to this store—

FRONTIER ARMY AND NAVY
WESTERN CLOTHES OUR SPECIALTY

"Hey, let's get your socks in here," Jack said. "It's probably run by some old cowboy whose ranch failed and he's selling western clothes now. I'll bet he's got some great stories about the Old West."

The store was a pretty big place. The goods were spread out on counters. Lots of floor space. I figured the rent per square foot of business space in San Francisco must be a lot cheaper than in New York, or else how could the guy cover his overhead.

We browsed around for a while. I picked up three pairs of identical dark blue socks. Then a short, thin, old man approached.

"You fellas find vat you're looking for?"

The accent was unmistakable. Gary Cooper he wasn't.

"Yeah," I said. "I only want some socks."

"Vell, you're a lucky man. You found vat you vanted."

He took the socks from me and motioned us to follow him. He put the socks on the counter next to the cash register to make it harder for us to change our mind.

He looked apprehensively at Hark. "Your dog. He's had lunch already?"

"Yeah," Jack said. "We just fed him a Big Mac."

"As long as he don't eat no Little Aarons. Cause that's me. Aaron. You want maybe some other colors, too. A nice green. Or a brown."

"No. I always buy the same color socks. Then if I lose one or two, I still can wear them."

He smiled. "You're Jewish."

"How'd you know?" Jack said.

"Only a Jew could buy socks like that. That's the way I used to buy them. How about you?" He said, picking up a pair of white socks and holding them out to Jack.

"No . . . " But then Jack noticed that the socks had no heels.

"What's the matter? You never saw socks like that?"

"They have no *heels*."

"They're *tube* socks."

"What if *you* have heels?"

"They stretch." He stretched the socks. "See. They fit anyone. How many you vant?" He turned to me, reaching into the box and pulling out a handful. "Seven? Eight?"

"I'll take one pair. Just to try them. Are they guaranteed?"

"Of course they're guaranteed. Guaranteed to tear." He put the rest of the socks away. "If they don't tear the first time you wear them, you bring them back and I'll give you a pair that *will* tear."

We laughed.

"You want maybe a tie?"

"I don't wear ties," Jack said.

But it was too late. The old man was already on the way to the tie department, motioning us to follow.

"What's the matter with you? You don't wear ties. There's a lot of places you can't get into without a tie. I got one here specially for you."

He dug down way behind some old boxes and came up with what must be The World's Worst Tie. It was huge, brown, with a picture of a guy on horseback painted on it in phosphorescent colors. It looked like it had been in the store since the gold rush. It didn't just have dust on it. It had mold. He held it up to Jack.

"Look at that! Is that a tie?"

It was hard to tell whether he was being serious or kidding.

I don't think he himself really knew. But when Jack took the tie from him and dusted it off, saying, "Just a minute while I get some of this penicillin off," the old man began to smile.

"Look, dat's me on the horse," he said, pointing to the picture on the tie. "I'm riding along, telling the Americans, 'De British are coming! De British are coming!'"

When we laughed, he relaxed out of his salesman role and put away the tie without a word. We were his buddies, now. My brother could do that to people when he wanted to. He could make them laugh and win them over in a second. I always wished he would do this in his writing (and do it more often in his life) instead of pushing his ideas about the Planet Opteema. It takes a lot of love and understanding to get on a person's trip and make him laugh, if you ask me. You have to be a human being.

"You boys work? Or you're on vacation?" the old man said, returning to the cash register.

"I'm an accountant."

He looked pleased. "And him?"

"I'm a rabbi from the Planet Opteema."

"He's a writer," I quickly explained, as I fished in my wallet for my Master Charge card.

"Oh, a writer." He turned toward Jack. "You read a lot?"

"I used to."

"You still read the Bible?"

"Sometimes."

"You read the New Testament?" Aaron asked, testing.

"You mean there's a *new* one?"

Aaron cracked up. He patted Jack on the back.

"Your brother's OK," he said to me, as he took my Master Charge card. "Rosen," he said, reading my name off the card. "The Chief Rabbi in Roumania was named Rosen. You think maybe you were related to him?"

"I don't know. My grandfather was the Chief Pants Presser in Odessa."

He smiled again. "You boys are OK. Remember, never lose your sense of humor. That's what our people learned in two thousand years. If you don't got an army, you gotta talk fast and tell a lot of jokes."

"I'll try not to," I said, as Aaron wrapped the socks.

As we left the store, Jack turned back to the old man. "Hey, Aaron, you ever hear of a town called Sebastopol?"

(Sebastopol was the nearest town to the place in the country, about sixty miles north of San Francisco, where we were going to live.)

"Sebastopol?"

"Yeah."

"Of course I know Sebastopol. In the Crimea. I remember when the son-of-a-bitch tsar took all the Jewish boys from our town to get them killed by the English in that crazy Crimean War. Tuey!" He spit on the floor. "Dat's what I think of Sebastopol. And the tsar. All those nice boys. What'd we ever get from his wars? Tuey!" He spit on the floor again.

"Wait a minute," I said. "That was over a hundred years ago. You couldn't remember that."

"Ah, what's the difference?" he said wearily, turning away. "There's always some tsar . . . "

He shuffled slowly over to a counter in the back of the store and we left him there, by himself, straightening out a display of Keds sneakers.

(The next day, when I tried on the pair of heel-less tube socks, my heel went right through the left one, tearing it irreparably. Aaron had told me the truth. They were guaranteed to tear and they did.)

We turned down Market Street and headed toward our meeting with Wheeler. Now I haven't told you about Wheeler yet, so I guess this is as good a time as any because he's going to be in the rest of the book. First of all, Wheeler wasn't his real name. His real name was Sandford Finkelstein. He didn't like his name, so everybody had called him Wheeler for as long as I could remember.

He lived in our building in The Bronx. When his father bought a liquor store in Harlem and began to make money, his family moved to Westchester but he was already a junior in high school by then and we stayed in touch. In fact, we were in the army together, Wheeler, and Jack, and I. (We joined up a month before the big escalation in Vietnam.)

After we got out, Wheeler disappointed his father, who wanted him to become a doctor or a lawyer, by going to business school with me. Then he made a pile of money in classy "Pawne Shoppes" he set up in the suburbs around New York City. He advertised on TV and really did it right (he has incredible energy). But just when he really got the business stabilized on a high level, he got bored, sold out to a big money-lending corporation (American Personal Finance, Inc.) that wanted to diversify, and he came to California to start a new life.

He decided to go to law school and (almost) be the person his father had wanted him to be. (More about that "almost" later.) And he bought a home in Sonoma County, just outside Sebastopol.

When we got back to the block the You-Go office was on, a young guy bummed a quarter off Jack. I wouldn't have given him a nickel. I checked the guy's shoes first. They were better than mine.

"Hey, you bums! Over here!"

It's Wheeler. Down the street, at the curb, in his station wagon. Out he jumps, all six-feet-one of him, slightly balding, long hair black as slate down to the broad shoulders that got him a tryout with the California Angels after he hit .301 in college and led the conference in home runs and was second in RBIs. (He played for three months in Class A baseball in Oklahoma, but he was hitting only .271 because his eyes weren't what they used to be and he couldn't see well enough under those minor-league lights, and he was bored, so he chucked it for the "Pawne Shoppes.")

In his station wagon, there's this pretty, sensitive-looking black woman. "What's this?" I say to myself. "Where's his wife, Becky?"

He bounds up to us with all that energy he has and hugs us, and Hark remembers him instantly and goes crazy over him, and then Wheeler brings us over to introduce us to the black lady. From up close I can see she has a cute round face, is just slightly plump, and her eyes twinkle beneath the African print kerchief she wears around her head.

"This is my wife, Becky Finkelstein," Wheeler announces, not able to hide his grin. "Née Rebecca Jackson of Lenox Avenue in Harlem."

(Remember that "almost" I put in above?)

Chapter 10

OK, OVER THE GOLDEN GATE BRIDGE and north on US 101, jammed into the Chevy wagon, Wheeler at the helm, the young Finkelstein lass at his side, with me on her right, Jack and Hark and the records packed into the back, Monsieur Joe Cockere on le tapedeck trying to get by with a little help from his friends just like the rest of us, as we're sailing along through acres of tall trees shading the loveliest, softest, pool-table green rug of grass, so inviting you just wanted to get out and roll all the way down a hill of the lush stuff, snakes and lizards be damned.

Wheeler is smiling that boyish grin he gets when he's happy and doesn't want to show it because he wants to hide his good heart and seem lawyer-tough (which he is anyway, along with being good-hearted) and he's talking nonstop: "So, when I was back east, I wanted to be an attorney and make a lot of dough and learn Romance languages, and take my clients out to these slick Manhattan restaurants and order the meals in French, and vacation in Italy and travel around looking at early Renaissance paintings by people like Giotto and Mantegna, but now that I've come out here I've kinda lost touch with Europe if you know what I mean. It seems so far away. I'm more in touch with the Orient."

"What's your aim now?" I asked.

"Now I want to make a lot of dough and take a client out

to a Hawaiian restaurant and order the meal in Hawaiian."

Jack had been unusually silent, there in the back. Which worried me. I thought I knew what it meant: Opteema Dreamin'.

And I was right, because once Wheeler quieted down, Jack took over and began to go on about California, and how great everything was going to be, and how the whole world was watching what happened right here, because California is the twenty-first century, and how even India and China are going to have to get their TVs and their housing developments and their freeways and divorces. ("In Russia, everyone already lives in the projects. Next step is the suburbs.") And, how, after that, when they get to where we're at now, they're going to have to look at California to find out where to go next, and that we were going to plant the seeds of a new world civilization based on a new relationship between people and nature, and a new relationship between people and other people, and that it might be difficult but there was no choice anyway because Pesseema was crumbling, and what we had to do was freak the Pesseemans out of their habitual ways of looking at the world, and steal their kids, and develop a way to live close to the land, and to teach ourselves to believe that the truth is what we will make happen, etc. etc. etc., all the way through Marin County and into Sonoma County, where the trees and houses were fewer, and there was more space.

Well, as he was gabbing away back there, Wheeler was picking up the pace of his driving, going about eighty-five, with the late Lee Morgan punching out a trumpet solo on the tapedeck and the sun just beginning to bed down for the night, and all of us flying on the speed that crystallizes in the vortex of a group of old friends meeting again to start a new life together, and Wheeler begins honking on the horn as we practically run up the back of a big lonesome Oldsmobile doing about fifty in the left of the two northbound lanes, and Wheeler is tailgating him and hitting the horn in little blurts of bee bee bedee in time with Art Blakey's drums, and the lone guy in the Olds is not only not moving, he's *slowing down* and shaking his fist at us, so Wheeler leans on the horn, but when the jerk still won't move, Wheeler cuts into the right lane, quickly, almost clipping the guy's taillight off, and jams it by him, giving him the finger as we pass.

So OK, we're mellow again, flying along at eighty-five, Wayne Shorter wailing on tenor over Bobby Timmons' choppy Bud Powell-style piano, when we look to our left, and there's the son-of-a-bitch in the Olds (fifty-five years old, cop-like) beside us, doing eighty-five and shaking his fist and shouting, so Wheeler loses it and begins to shout back as the guy hits the gas and gets in front of us and *slows down again* and Mrs. Finkelstein is telling Wheeler to slow down too, but it's too late, the dude has gotten Wheeler's Irish up (Wheeler is one-half Irish on his neighbor's side, as are all us Bronx guys from Highbridge). So Wheeler is trying to pass but the jerk is *between* the two lanes now, swerving left and right to keep us back, and I'm agreeing with Mrs. Finkelstein's self-preservation demands but Jack is in the back, jamming, "Get him, Wheeler! Get him! He ain't getting away with that on a Bronx guy," and I know we're in for it because Jack is getting Wheeler on his "Bronx guy" trip and there's no one more into being a Bronx guy than a guy who's left The Bronx for greener pastures.

Anyhow, I'm just sitting there, thanking God that the guy ahead of us is blocking the whole highway and at least we're stuck behind him, when suddenly madman Wheeler floors it and we're passing the big Olds *on the center mall* and I look at the guy as we shoot by him and he's not even shaking his fist—he's as dumbfounded as I am, and you can tell by the look on his face that he knew Wheeler was a madman, but he didn't think Wheeler was *that much* of a madman.

Well, we get by the guy and emerge alive, and I finish saying my Jewish rosaries to the Moses of the Freeways (Robert Moses?), but just as we're beginning to relax, we feel a bump and look and the crazy cop-like guy is on our left, and he's running alongside of us, practically foaming at the mouth, and he's bumped us to the right, so I quickly say, "Wheeler! This guy is nuts! Let him go. He's an *American*. He doesn't understand tragedy!"

But, of course, Wheeler makes a short, quick swing toward the left, bumping the guy toward the mall. Well, this gets the guy (and Wheeler) even crazier, and now Jack is yelling out of the window at the guy, "Fuck off! You jerk!" and then, as we pass a sign on the right that says:

CALIFORNIA HIGHWAY PATROL
EXIT 1 MILE

the inevitable happens. The guy is flashing a badge at us and pointing to the sign and signalling us to get off at the state cops' house.

SLAMMERVILLE!

But Wheeler is shouting back at the guy, "OK, Fucker! You asked for it!" and just as I'm saying, "Wheeler! This guy has a badge!" and Mrs. Finkelstein has a look on her face which is the horror-filled outward expression of God-knows-what black inner visions of police station nightmares, we approach the single lane, 30 MPH, exit, and Wheeler and the guy are flying at it at 60, *parallel* to each other, each barely on the road, and they race across the empty parking lot, slam into the curb next to each other, neither even bothering to park, and Wheeler and the guy race into the CHP headquarters, Jack and I behind them, Becky not leaving the car, and we get through the door just in time to see Wheeler and the guy rush up to the desk and arrest each other.

Chapter 11

TO MAKE A LONG STORY SHORT, cooler heads prevailed. (The fact that the cooler heads in question were those of men wearing California Highway Patrol uniforms, and packing big revolvers on their hips, didn't hurt their case any.)

As soon as Wheeler and the other guy had grabbed each other and began to shout at the desk sergeant in a weird, excited, cacophonous, American, staccato, scat duet that no one could understand, three other cops came running up and quieted them, but even then no one could piece together the story. I was worried for Wheeler's sake. I was wondering how he could expect to get admitted to the bar with a "Willfully and Purposefully Crashing Into a Cop" scene on his record.

Then the cop guy calmed down enough to say he wanted to make a citizen's arrest.

Well, once he said that "citizen's," Jack and I threw each other a relieved glance. We suddenly saw that Wheeler had a sane fix on the situation, and just as the other cops fade back to their desks, and the sergeant says, "Well, that's a complicated procedure . . . But it is possible . . . , " and he gets up from his desk, "If you insist, I'll go in the back and get the forms," and Wheeler shoots in, "Well, Sarge, you better get a couple extra, because I'm going to charge this dude with 'Impersonating an Officer of the Law,' and he's gonna get put in the jug and lose his job at whatever Safeway he defends," and the sergeant goes into the back room and the jerk turns white and starts to stutter, and we know we're home free.

The guy says, "Well, I . . . I . . . ," and Wheeler says, "I know a dime-store security badge when I see one," and the guy says, "I . . . I'll be right back," and he checks out to the parking lot, and when the sergeant returns with the forms, we see the guy in the Olds tear-assing out of the lot onto the freeway.

Well, by this time, Jack's calmed down, and he talks to the sergeant, and there, right on the spot, and without the guy to contradict him, he makes up a novel about us and the guy that exonerates us and satisfies the sergeant in the way that only a novelist can, because, as Jack told me a hundred times, a novelist gets paid to lie, and the secret of good novelists is that their work *isn't* autobiographical but only *seems* that way because, in a world of liars, to get paid for lying you have to be pretty damn good at it, and, like I said before, Jack was.

When we got outside, Wheeler's station wagon was there, with all the records in it, but with no sign of Hark or Becky. This puzzled us. Then Jack called, "Hark!" and out he bounded from behind a tree at the edge of the woods, just beyond the parking lot, with a frightened-looking Becky following.

"Damn!" she said to Wheeler. "Are you crazy? You're gonna get locked up for sure one of these days."

But Wheeler just laughed at how she was trying to look so mad as she stormed up to us, when even Jack and I could see she was smiling inside because Wheeler was free and she didn't have to deal with the police.

"Hey," Wheeler said to her, laughing, nodding toward Hark, "I thought you didn't like dogs."

"I like dogs a hell of a lot better than I like *woods*," she said, sternly, moving back into her seat in the station wagon.

But the smile snuck out around the corners of her mouth.

We had to go back a couple exits (Wheeler had passed our exit in the heat of "The Great Cop Race") and when we finally got on two-lane Route 116 and slowed down, the sun had just set and it was my favorite time of day, when everything is so quiet the whole world seems like an outdoor library.

But it was still light enough to see the five teenagers

laughing at the girl driving the old Chevy that swerved crazily as it slowly came toward us in the approaching lane. She was trying to drive the car while looking at the road through these big binoculars.

Jack and I were silently excited as we entered Sebastopol, a town of 4,004 people. Wheeler drove down the main street, stopped briefly at one of the town's two stoplights, and then pulled into the parking lot outside the huge Safeway, where we waited while Becky went inside to buy a chicken for dinner.

"This used to be a movie theater," Wheeler said.

"*This?*" I said.

"Not the building. The site. They tore down the old Analy Theater to build the big new Safeway last year."

"I hate that kind of thing," Jack said. "I wish I could have seen it once. Was it real old?"

"Yeah . . ."

"It's too bad we missed it," Jack said.

We could see Becky through the large Safeway windows. She had paid for her chicken, but an old man wearing a *yarmulke* (a Jewish skull cap) was talking heatedly at her and gesticulating with his hands. He was wearing a suit without a tie.

"That old guy bothering Becky?" Jack said.

"Nah, that's only Rabinowitz," Wheeler said. "He's the local purist at the synagogue. Nothing's orthodox enough for him."

I slid over next to Wheeler as Becky came back into the station wagon.

"What's Rabinowitz want now?" Wheeler said.

"Oh, he's on another campaign . . . This time he wants the kids to wear clothes when they swim in the coed sessions in the pool."

"Are you serious?" I said.

"People are pretty cool about that stuff out here," Wheeler said. "Everyone takes saunas together and we all swim at the nude beach up on the Russian River, about seven miles north of here."

"You see," Jack said to me, as Wheeler pulled out into Main Street, "it's already Opteema out here, but the people don't realize it yet . . . It's like the Buddha said, the only problem is ignorance . . . "

All the stores in town were closed except for a couple taverns. The streets were empty. It had cooled quickly since the sun had set. A brisk breeze blew and it seemed unnaturally quiet. We passed through the shopping area and then turned right up a hill.

"You're associated with the Jewish Center?" I asked Becky.

"She assists the social director," Wheeler said. "I told you on the phone."

"Oh . . . right . . . "

"It's OK," Becky said, gently, noticing that I was embarrassed. "Everyone's a little surprised when they hear."

"But how did you come to be Jewish?"

"It was my father I guess . . . Do you know Izzy's Furniture Store on 125th Street in Harlem?"

"About two blocks east of the Apollo Theater?" Jack said.

"That's the one."

"I know that store," I said. "The one with the big electric "SALE" sign that's always on in the window."

"Your father worked at Izzy's?" Jack said.

"My father *owned* Izzy's."

"*What?*" I said.

"Your father bought out Izzy?" Jack said.

"My father *was* Izzy."

Wheeler laughed at our surprise. "His name was Isaac Jackson," he explained.

"My father had this idea that the black people *wanted* to buy from Jews. So he called his store 'IZZY'S' and he pretended he only worked there."

"He made a lot of money," Wheeler laughed.

"Are you serious?" I said.

"It's true," Wheeler said.

"In California anything is possible," Jack said.

"My father believed that black people had to learn how to get out of the ghetto from the Jews. I think it was rebelling against this that made my brother a black-power revolutionary for a while."

"Your brother is nuts . . . " Wheeler said.

"No he's not . . . That's not fair. He *was* a little anti-

Semitic for a while, but since he came back from Togoland in the Peace Corps, he's mellowed out . . . He's into black capitalism now."

Wheeler turned down a dark country lane. "I think it was in rebellion against her brother that Becky converted to Jewish."

"What'd your father think about all this?" Jack said.

"Well, I guess we both went a little beyond what he'd expected . . . But he was nice about it. He paid for my brother to go to Howard University. And I went to Brandeis."

"*You* went to Brandeis?" I said.

"It's not so strange. Angela Davis went there, too."

"And your father? Is he still running Izzy's?" Jack said.

"He retired . . . He and my mother live in Miami now."

After we unloaded our stuff in Wheeler's big barn of a house, and Becky cooked us an excellent soul food dinner—gefilte fish, and then a nice roast chicken with kasha varnishkes and carrot tsimmis—and we listened to some of their records—Becky played Mendelssohn during dinner and then Stan Getz, Wheeler played some Theolonius Monk and John Coltrane while we sipped his Remy Martin—Wheeler told us the surprise he had been holding back for just this perfect moment: the property next to his house was for sale.

"It's an acre of nice land, practically surrounded by apple orchards. Sebastopol's famous Gravenstein apples."

"Unbelievable!" Jack said. "We can buy it and live in a teepee."

"It has a house on it," Wheeler laughed. "An older redwood house, fronting on the same road as mine. The road dead-ends about three hundred feet past the house. So it's real rural and quiet. No one ever comes up that way. You'll hardly know the automobile's been invented."

"Seclusion! Orchards! Our own land!" Jack said.

And the price was right, too. Unbelievably right compared to my New Yorker's idea of what property was worth. And I could meet the down payment out of my savings from my accounting job.

"It's almost too good to be true," I said.

"Look out, Thomas Jefferson!" Jack shouted. He leaped up and began to do a mad Mick Jagger dance, throwing his elbows out to the sides like a basketball rebounder. "Here we come! American yeoman farmers."

"Forty acres and a mule," Becky said, smiling.

"Opteema, we are here!" Jack said.

"We haven't seen the property yet," I said.

"Are you kidding? It's perfect!" Jack said.

"We don't know anything about property."

"We know the difference between Property and Land, daddy. On Opteema, we don't have *Property*. We have Land. . . . And this is Land out here, Jerr. *Land!*"

Well, even after all the cognac we'd drunk, I still couldn't really see the difference. But as it turned out, it really was a bargain. In fact, the very next day, I learned we were going to get even more than we bargained for with the property.

We got the Battapaglias.

Chapter 12

ALL FOUR OF THEM.

(Actually there were two Battapaglias, a Franklin, and a Moholy-Nagy, but I'll explain this in a minute.)

(In fact, it turned out there were *two* Franklins:

1—Grandma Bessie Franklin. Gentle matriarch of the Battapaglia clan.

2—Franklin Stove. Which, logically enough, was the name Nectarine Battapaglia gave to the Franklin stove that was located in the old, shingled, redwood house we were going to buy from her mother. "Let's give Franklin his dinner," she would say when it was time to put on the evening logs.)

But, to make this clear, let me list the Battapaglia clan:

1—Grandma Bessie Franklin. (Nectarine's grandmother.) Age 88. Born in Arkansas. Came to California in the 1890s in a covered wagon. (Her family couldn't afford to ride the train.) When we arrived, she was living by herself in a huge, monster, air-conditioned, aluminum and plastic mobile home, located on an acre lot on the far side of the lot we were to buy. (Wheeler's lot was on the other side of our property.)

2—Laura Lee Franklin Battapaglia. (Nectarine's mother.) Bessie Franklin's daughter. When she was in her twenties, she had moved to Hollywood, where she eventually came to own several beauty parlors. She married Dominick Battapaglia, an "estimator" for Lockheed Aircraft, born in Chicago. After eleven years, they divorced, and Dominick changed jobs and moved back to Chicago. At that time, Laura Lee turned over her business to the care of her assistant and bought, from her mother, the acre and the house (her childhood home) that we were to buy, and she moved back to Sebastopol with her three children (Nectarine and her two younger brothers). Grandma Bessie Franklin moved out of the old house and into the mobile home on the adjoining acre. After three months, Laura Lee moved back to Hollywood. Her three kids moved to Chicago to live with their father.

3—Nectarine Battapaglia. Age 28. Her name at birth wasn't Nectarine, but that's the name she chose when she moved back to California from Chicago, so let's honor her wish and leave it at that. Born in Hollywood. Spent her teenage years in Chicago, where she practically raised her two younger brothers, Angie the Janitor, six years younger than she, and Luigi the Hippie, nine years younger. When she was nineteen, she entered the University of Chicago in the humanities program (the "Great Books Program"). She graduated at the age of twenty-three with a B.A. Her unofficial major was art history.

Then she moved to New York with a Hungarian-Jewish sculptor who called himself Gaudier-Brzeska Moholy-Nagy. (His friends called him "Marc.") They did the art trip for a while, lived on Avenue C on no dollars a month (or at least, Nectarine later told me, it seemed that way). She had a son, they named him Jimi (after Jimi Hendrix), the sculptor panicked and disappeared, and Nectarine moved to California with little Jimi, into the old family house in Sebastopol, living there on welfare, next to her grandmother in the mobile home on the next lot.

4—Jimi Franklin Battapaglia Moholy-Nagy. (Nectarine's son.) Age three. With a wonderful, outgoing, overflowing spirit, and Nectarine's soft blonde hair down to his shoulders and sometimes over his eyes. He could be a lot of fun. He could sometimes be a pain in the ass. We all liked him.

But to get back to the story, on our first morning in Sonoma County, we woke up to Eric Clapton and roses. Clapton screaming over Cream on "White Room" and roses in bloom on three exploding bushes in Wheeler's backyard just outside our window. Our room was bright with east-morning sunshine and the air was so fresh it smelled like new white sheets on a clean bed, with beige-colored blankets and a mahogany headboard.

Becky fixed us this nice breakfast of lox and eggs. (We didn't like lox, but we didn't have the heart to tell her.)

While we were eating (to an early Chet Baker record—"Chet Baker Sings"—Wheeler knew Jack loved Chet Baker's trumpet solos and romanticized Chet's junkie downfall and his years in an Italian stone dungeon-prison with his cell lighted only by a twenty-watt bulb. When my brother would meet a woman he liked, he would always play his Chet Baker records and tell her his version of Chet's life, the brilliant young artist who fell into an abortive trip before all his promise could be fully born, and after a while, it was almost like he was telling his own story, and he had become the young, tragically impaired artist, too sensitive to live in so harsh a reality as this one, and the woman would usually see this, and fall in love with Jack, but this wasn't the reason he told his Chet Baker story to her. No, those love affairs just seemed to happen. He really loved Chet Baker's romantic story *as a story*. Just as he loved Hampton Hawes' story, too, the other brilliant young jazzman imprisoned for drugs who was rotting away in a Texas prison until John F. Kennedy pardoned him in an act, which Jack said, would redound to the late president's credit long after the dumb Cuban missile crisis had faded into the lost graveyard of Pesseeman realpolitick.) Anyhow, as I began to say at the beginning of this sentence, as we were eating, in walked this tall, slim, soft-haired, seaweed-blonde woman with a little boy who looked just like her and a little girl with light-dark skin and a wiry Afro hairdo.

When Jack saw them, he fell over backwards onto the floor, chair and all, almost knocking over the whole table which Wheeler grabbed, just in time, with his quick, third-baseman's hands. As I helped Jack up, I could see it in his eyes: Opteema. I knew we were in for trouble.

"Botticelli!" was all he said as I reached down to him. His eyes were looking spaced-upwards, toward (or through) the ceiling. "Botticelli!"

At first I was confused, but when we got him back together

with his seat at the table, and Becky introduced us to Nectarine and Jack dumbly stared at her, transfixed by her face, I realized what he was talking about, because she did look a little like Botticelli's Venus, except for her witch eyes which were slightly askew and looked like they'd been added by a cubist who had tried to imitate Botticelli but had fallen back into his own style on the eyes.

She certainly was lovely looking, in any case, with her soft, damp-seeming hair, and her nose just slightly too large, but this made her even more charming in the way she moved through her flaw, in the way Carmen Miranda's nose was too large, but added to her charm because it made you realize how much she had done with what she had been given.

Jack had literally flipped over her. Well, for most people, to flip over a lady, or to see her as like an ideal figure in the work of a great painter, would not be dangerous. But I knew that when he was on "Opteema," my brother didn't think in terms of "like." (If I were a writer instead of an accountant,* I would say that for Jack there were no similes. Only metaphors. For him, Nectarine wasn't *like* a Botticelli. She *was* a Botticelli! And this is not an exaggeration. Really! That's the way his mind worked.)

So, as I said, when I saw that look in his eyes, I knew I was in for trouble. To me, Nectarine was a nice looking woman, but there was something about her that made me uneasy.

When Jack calmed down a little, Becky introduced us to Nectarine's son, Jimi, and to Becky's daughter, Shoshanna.

"Your daughter?" I said.

"From her first marriage," Wheeler said.

"I guess I thought Wheeler had told you." Becky removed the girl's checked sweater. "Shoshanna is Hebrew. It's like Suzanna in English. But I guess you knew that."

"No, I don't really know any Hebrew."

"Weren't you bar-mitzvahed when you were thirteen?"

"Yeah, but we never really went to Hebrew school. The

---

*Oh, come off it!
  Dr. F.

rabbi would always say, 'Everything has to have a maker, right? A shoe has a shoemaker. A bottle has a bottle maker. Well, God is the One who made the world.' And Jack would say, 'Then who made God?' and I would say, 'Yeah, who was the Godmaker?' And then the rabbi would get mad and throw us out of school and we would go play stickball in the street."

"How old were you?" Nectarine said.

"About eleven, I guess."

"Too much!" she said. "Getting into hot water with the rabbis on theological grounds at the age of eleven!" She smeared some cream cheese on a bagel for little Jimi. "I don't even think Spinoza got kicked out until he was in his thirties."

"I think it was really the stickball. We didn't want to be saved. We wanted to play for the Yankees."

At this point I looked toward Jack, ready for him to do a couple funny stickball stories, but I could see his eyes were still unfocused. He wasn't following our conversation. He was marveling at the "miracle" that had brought a figure from a Renaissance painting into his life.

Becky handed the bagel to Jimi and said to me, "But you *were* bar-mitzvahed?"

"Yeah. When we were twelve and a half, our parents got us this renegade Hebrew teacher. He gave us records of him singing the prayers we had to learn. Every time we learned a new section of a record he'd take us to Palisades Amusement Park in New Jersey so we could go on the Tilt-A-Whirl. He had the worst voice in the western hemisphere, but it worked."

"The bar mitzvah went OK?"

"No one knew we didn't have the foggiest idea of what we were saying." I smiled. "The best part was at the reception that night in the basement of the synagogue. Everyone was dressed to kill and making believe they were these really ritzy people at the Metropolitan Opera, when my cousin Frieda from Brooklyn, who weighed 284 pounds, got drunk, and passed out, and pissed on her gown, and it took four strong men almost a half an hour to get her up the narrow curved staircase out of the basement."

"That's true," Wheeler said. "I was there."

"And years later, when I *did* go to the Metropolitan

Opera, it seemed like just another bar mitzvah to me."

"Well," Wheeler said, turning toward Jack, "if we can arouse Bernard Berenson over here, maybe we can get our asses over next door to look at Nectarine's house."

When Jack realized we were all looking at him, he came back to reality and smiled, and he helped us clean off the table. Wheeler explained to Nectarine that we might be interested in buying her mother's property.

Becky seemed relieved to see Jack back in the world again. But I wasn't. I knew him better than she did. I knew it was too late.

Chapter 13

BECKY LED US TO THE DOOR. She opened the three locks and we followed her outside.

"Do you need all these locks around here?" I asked.

"I told her no," Wheeler said, "but she won't listen."

"I didn't put any bars on the windows, did I?" Becky said.

She reached down and opened the heavy lock on the welded steel gate that joined the two ends of the seven-foot-high metal fence.

"She doesn't just like locks, she collects them," Wheeler said. "I'm not kidding. She has dozens of them."

"Someday I'm going to go to England," Becky said. "They have the world's biggest padlock there. They say it's almost two feet high."

Wheeler and I followed Jack and Nectarine and the kids through the gate. We turned to the left on the quiet, country, blacktop road. Becky made sure the gate was closed securely behind us. I never got to know Becky very well, and I find it hard to say much about her. She was an extremely good, decent, reliable person, but sometimes I felt that in becoming the person she was, she might have suppressed the most interesting part of herself.

"My mother's staying with us for a few days to sell the property," Nectarine said, as we walked past the cream-colored Cadillac parked up against the seven-foot-high fence that was similar to Becky's except this one had three strands of barbed wire on top. We passed through the open gate and climbed up the five warped-wood steps onto the porch of the old redwood house. Where the front door should have been, there was just a heavy khaki blanket hung on two big nails.

"But, there's no door!" I said.

"It came loose last winter, so I chopped it up and burned it in Franklin one night," Nectarine said, laughing. "I guess I was a little high at the time."

Becky looked at me and shrugged her shoulders.

"We don't need a door anyhow," Nectarine said. "Not with mother's Auschwitz fence around the whole place."

"But you never close the gate," Becky said.

"No one steals in the country," Nectarine said.

"Too much!" Jack said.

Wheeler laughed. We followed Nectarine into the house. She said, "You'll be surprised at the inside. The outside of the house is in the country. The inside's in Hollywood."

And the house *was* like two houses. Outside, it seemed a ramshackle affair, peeling shingles like a skin disease, pine cones plopped all over on the slightly slanted roof, the porch on a tilt, the white washed off its boards by weather and time, and a kind of mildew (or penicillin) on them that made them seem like they were underwater at high tide (although even I knew the Pacific Ocean was about ten miles away).

Inside, though, it *was* Hollywood. The whole interior had been modernized. Nectarine's mother had had walls knocked out and everything was so pinkified that if Senator Joe McCarthy had been alive, Laura Lee would have been under investigation. The walls had been painted pink in every room. The floor was covered with wall-to-wall fluffy white carpeting that looked like it had been sewn together from the pelts of English sheepdogs. The windows in the living room and bedrooms were covered by heavy pink drapes. The windows in the bathroom and kitchen were screened by these strings of pink Woolworth beads of different sizes. The central living room light on the ceiling was surrounded by an upside-down wedding cake fixture of milky plastic pendules. And the bathroom walls were covered with a wallpaper that featured rows of pink poodles all smiling like they had been accidentally locked in Tiffany's at closing time and had spent the night trying on diamond-studded collars and leashes.

When Laura Lee came out of the bedroom, I expected her to be pink as well, but she wasn't. She was orange. Her pump slippers were pink, but her robe was shocking orange and her hair was a darker shade of orange. She was thin. There was something scattered about her. She slurred her speech, as if she had been born in Phenobarb, California, rather than Sebastopol. Perhaps she had seen *Streetcar Named Desire* one too many times and had been invested with the spirit of Blanche DuBois.

But Laura Lee was tougher than Blanche. She apologized for the condition of the house, and for her appearance, told us she had a heart condition, popped a couple downers of one kind or another, and lead us out around the property, a really terrific acre of land, sloping down to a creek under oak trees at the bottom fence, behind which the land climbed back up into an empty hill of high grass. From the creek, you couldn't see any houses besides hers and the big mobile home on the next lot, and to a couple city boys like us, it seemed like a kind of Eden.

To Jack it was "the first acre on the Planet Opteema." When Nectarine reached into a pocket she had sewn onto her dress and pulled out a big bomber joint and lit up, I knew she wasn't about to disagree. I didn't know much about buying property, but I trusted Wheeler when he whispered in my ear, "Take it. It's a steal!" Still, I tried to concentrate on the practical aspects of the matter, and to try to keep Wheeler away from the dope long enough to clue me in on what they were, since I had never lived in anything but an apartment in my whole life.

We walked under the big oak tree next to the creek, where I was struck by what looked like six tiny headstones on the ground. I walked over and sure enough they had writing on them. As I bent over to read the first (BELOVED FOU FOU), Laura Lee explained, "Oh, that's right now, you'll have to promise not to disturb my doggies' resting place before I'll consider selling you the propery. I won't sell to anyone who might disturb my doggies' rest."

I read the names and dates on the stones. "They all died on

the same day. Was there an epidemic or something?"

"No. I put them to sleep."

I turned away and pretended to look at the big tree above us. I didn't know what to say.

"My poodles killed sheep. I built this big fence around the property. It cost me over a thousand dollars at Sears. But they kept getting out anyhow . . . So I had to put them to sleep. It seemed the kindest thing to do . . . I couldn't have kept them tied up. That would've been too cruel . . . And I couldn't give them away . . . They would've died of loneliness for me . . ."

"How did you do it?"

"Do what?"

"Put them to sleep."

"With my former husband's forty-five."

At this moment, Jack rolled down the hill toward us, followed by Jimi and Shoshanna, who were trying to roll on the grass in the same way he did. Right from the start, I could see that Nectarine dug him. And now that she had finished smoking her bomber, she seemed to dig him even more. Especially when he gave us a little speech about crystals, and how this acre was the seed around which the crystals of a new planet would grow.

Jack and the kids ran back up the hill to try again.

"Are you and Jimi going back to L.A. when the property is sold?" I asked Nectarine, as we ambled back up toward the house.

"No . . . I don't really know what I'll do . . . I don't really feel like going anywhere . . ."

She didn't seem very concerned. Later, I would learn that no one in California seems all that concerned about the future. I think it's because there's no winter. And no Bowery. So they aren't subject to the New York nightmare of winding up on the Bowery in the winter. In California, if you don't have a house you can always sleep in your car. And there's always someone to give you a joint or two, so before you know it you're sleeping in the Ritz-With-A-Steering-Wheel.

Up near the top of the hill, we met Jack rolling down it. He popped up and said to Laura Lee, "This place is great! Just great! We'll take it. When can we move in?"

"Why, tomorrow is OK, I guess . . . We can go to the title

office in the morning . . . I'll sell you the furniture if you like . . . I think I could drive down to Los Angeles in the afternoon." She batted her eyelashes. "Oh, you gentlemen are so nice to transact business so expeditiously . . . That's the way gentlemen used to do business in the South. My ancestors were from the South," she said, her accent getting more southern. "Oh, why don't we go tell mother . . . "

She turned to the left at the old wooden flagpole with the tattered American flag on it, and headed toward a gate in the fence that led to the huge mobile home. We followed.

"What'll you do tomorrow?" I asked Nectarine.

"Oh, I don't know . . . This next acre belongs to my grandmother. Maybe Jimi and I'll borrow a couple sleeping bags and sleep on her property for a while, down near the creek."

"But suppose it rains."

"You gentlemen really *have* just come here," Laura Lee said. "It's not going to rain."

"Not till the fall, at least," Wheeler said.

Bessie Franklin's mobile home was set in front of a backdrop of spindly apple trees that blanched out in a flurry of white blossoms, so soft and fluffy and full they took my breath away.

It was as good as seeing the Pasadena Rose Parade on a terrific color TV.

Bessie was seated on the vinyl couch in her living room, watching a soap opera on her TVs. I could see four of them from where I stood. Sears' color portables. One in the kitchenette, one in each of the two corners of the living room that faced grandma's couch, and one I could see looking back at me down the hallway from in her bedroom. All of them were turned to the same show.

She rose to greet us. She could hardly walk. She pushed a "walker," a kind of four-legged support, in front of her as she moved step by tiny step toward us. Except for the mobile home, from the looks of her, her simple gray dress and gray hair and her plain black shoes, she seemed like she could still be back in Arkansas.

"I can't get around too much," she said. "It's my Arthur-itis."

Well, of course, that knocked Jack out. I could see that

he had fallen in love with her on the spot, with her color TVs and her "Arthur-itis."

"Don't you worry about a thing, Mrs. Franklin," he said. "You're invited. In fact, you're there already." And then, to me, "The crystal just doubled, Jerr. Two acres now."

Mrs. Franklin didn't know what he was talking about. But I could see she liked him. They smiled at each other. Jack shook her hand when she offered it to him.

We talked for a while with Bessie, mostly about the land and the history of her life on it (her late husband had built the house we were buying), and how she had come across in a covered wagon (Jack got her to expand on this), and how she only wished she could get around a bit more, and how she was glad a person like Jack was buying the land who would appreciate it.

As we headed back to Wheeler's house, leaving Nectarine with her mother at the gate, Jack turned to her and asked if she could come over that night. He wanted to play some of his Chet Baker records for her. When she said, "Sure," I felt like I had gone to see someone off on a train, and it had started to move while I was still on board, and that now there was no getting off until we got to the next stop.

And I didn't have the faintest idea of where that stop would be, or when it would come.

Chapter 14

THE WEDDING WAS SET for the following Saturday night. Nectarine had suggested Friday night but Becky wouldn't have it then because Friday night was the beginning of the Jewish sabbath.

And the wedding was to be in Becky's house. Completely paid for and arranged by Becky and Wheeler as a wedding present to my brother and his lovely bride and her lovely son. And her lovely grandmother. And to her two lovely brothers, if they showed up. And to God knows who else came with the deal.

We had bought the house on the morning of the day after we first looked at it. When we went to the title company to put the deal on paper, Laura Lee quietly raised the price we had agreed on by five hundred bucks. Nectarine and Jack were too much in love to notice. I was about to protest, but Wheeler, who was right on top of the deal and saw exactly what had happened, walked up to me and said quickly, out of the side of his mouth, in carny talk, "Tearsake it, anywears. It's a stearseal!" So I went along with Laura Lee, and she was so grateful she decided to throw in the pink drapes for free. (When she heard about the wedding, she decided she had left them as a wedding present.)

She couldn't stay for the wedding. Had to get back to L.A. Which was OK with me.

The drapes came in handy immediately. Nectarine pulled them down and sewed them up with some purple satin material she had found down by the railroad tracks to make a "Lord Krishna" costume for Jimi to wear to carry the ring down the aisle. Well, when he tried it on, he looked more like some little kid version of the guy on the Joyva Halvah wrappers to me, but, as they say, Krishna comes in many forms. (Unfortunately, most of them have blue skin.)

Anyhow, as long as she didn't ask me to dress up as one of Krishna's milkmaids, what the hell did I care?

I got nothing against anyone else's ikons. Even if the only ikon I believe in is Ikon Tina Turner.

OK. The wedding. How can I get it into words? Maybe I should start by describing the first guest. He came in the door at dusk, wearing these German-type Bermuda shorts, held up by suspenders, with no shirt on underneath. He had dark hair and a beard. He was carrying a bow and he had arrows in an arrow holder strapped to his back.

At first I thought it was some strange kind of hippie holdup—that the guy was going to grab the wedding presents and run off into the woods—so I backed off until I saw by the way Wheeler walked up to him that the guy was on our side.

"This is Adam-Zohar," Wheeler said. I shook the guy's hand. I expected the guy to give me some weird Adam-Zohar shake, but he shook American. So the shake went off OK. It turned out he was from Scranton, Pennsylvania.

"How come the bow and arrow?" I said.

"Oh, I hunt for my meat. I won't eat any meat unless I kill it myself with the bow and arrow."

I was going to say, "Then you must be pretty much a vegetarian," because I couldn't picture a guy from Scranton making it as Natty Bumpo stalking game through people's backyards, but I figured what the hell, the guy's not bothering me, why should I bother him?

I came here to learn, didn't I?

Besides, the guy might very well be a vegetarian, but he was armed. And if you think all vegetarians are harmless, you should check out the Hindus in India. They don't kill cows. They only kill Moslems who kill cows.

I always watch out with vegetarians. You never know

when they're gonna get hungry for meat.

Anyhow, after Adam-Zohar, the other guests began to arrive and they were a mixed bag, I'll tell you. There was Grandma Franklin, shuffling in behind her table-crutch, and a bunch of Wheeler's law school friends from San Francisco (he was finishing his first year there) and a lot of the Americans who lived in the neighborhood, some people from the synagogue, and a large number of the Zohar people who had probably come to Northern California for the same reasons as my brother Jack did—to find some kind of Opteema to put up against the land of their birth which, I guess, they felt had rejected them.

It was my first California party, and as a Bronx accountant I have to admit that I was surprised to see that right on the bar in Wheeler's huge living room he had set two large silver trays. One had these expensive crystal glasses filled with good local Korbel champagne (I hadn't known that some of the best wines in America came from the area around Sonoma County) and on the other silver tray, displayed in neat rows, dozens and dozens of fat joints.

Nectarine had spent all afternoon rolling them out of half of the pound of marijuana Wheeler had bought from a dark guy named Jose.

When Jose had come with the dope at noon, Nectarine pulled me off to the side. "He's an angel," she whispered.

"He looks more like a Chicano to me."

"No, he's an angel."

Becky overheard, and later she told me that he had only taken the name "Jose" because he was a dealer and he wanted to keep the law off his trail. "He's actually a Jewish guy from New Jersey," she said. "His name is really Irwin."

Well, I didn't know what to believe, but when everyone started sampling the Korean dope that Jose was passing around, I joined in (so as not to appear rude), and, I have to admit it, after a while he did seem a little like an angel. I kept waiting for his street-tough dealer personality to come out. But it never did.

Jack and Jose and Wheeler and I were moving the furniture around to get the room ready for the party that night, and all Jose kept saying was, "Wow! Will my partner be happy! I'm some salesman. I go out with sixteen lids of dope and I sell them all at my first stop."

Wheeler said, "He pays a hundred and forty dollars for a pound, and he divides it into sixteen big lids, and goes from door to door to all his friends' houses, and when he's sold them all he has a hundred and forty-four dollars."

"This guy's my kind of businessman," Jack said, putting his arm around Jose who beamed. "We come from the same planet. Right, amigo?"

Jose continued to smile.

"I had a friend once who sold shoes," I said. "He bought them for ten bucks a pair and he sold them for nine."

"How could he stay in business?" Wheeler asked.

"He made it up on volume."

Wheeler cracked up. Jose, I noticed, just kept his consistent glow.

"I guess angels just don't understand business," I said to Jack, later, when we were alone.

"If they've been around since the Middle Ages, they must be doing something right," he said.

Anyhow, to get back to the wedding, I'd been to parties where people got pretty loaded, but I'd never seen a mix of people like that night where some of the folks seemed as innocent as they could be of the fact that the other folks were, as rapidly and efficiently as possible, getting themselves blown out of their minds. One thing I should mention about these Californians—or, rather, two things that I learned that night and that I still believe to be true:

1—They'll never say no to free wine and/or dope. Never! Morning, noon, or night, if there's a chance for a party, they'll swing with it.

2—They never worry about limits. If you give them a joint, they'll smoke it. If you give them five joints, they'll smoke them. If you were to put them in a marijuana field with a carton of cigarette papers, it's good-bye-pork pie—they'll be back in a year.

I figured most of the people at the party were Nectarine's friends, but I found out later they were actually friends of Wheeler's. Everyone liked Nectarine, but I learned that she tended to stay pretty much by herself on her little Opteema-acre, stoned all day, with Jimi and Shoshanna.

There wasn't much conversation at the party (which was OK with me) and what talk there was had to be shouted over the band that Wheeler had hired—"Myron and His Valley-Mountain Boys." A country music band led by a guy named Myron Nadelbaum from Silver Spring, Maryland. I talked to them during the break and it turned out Myron had met two of the other musicians at the University of Maryland. They were from Baltimore. Doug, the country fiddler, was from Palo Alto. His father was a professor of English at Stanford. Joey the black drummer was from Newark, New Jersey. He told me he wanted to get back east. "I have kids back there, man. I haven't seen them in two years."

"Oh, you're a family man. Where are they?"

"The kids?"

"Yeah."

"Let's see (he began to count on his fingers) . . . There's one in Pennsylvania . . . There's one in Maryland . . . two in New York . . . and . . . and one in Massachusetts . . ."

He took a long toke on a joint. "Oh, wait a minute now . . . Did I say two in New York and one in Massachusetts?"

"I think so."

"No . . . No, that's not it, man . . . It's *one* in New York and *two* in Massachusetts . . . How much does that make?"

He took another long toke.

"Five, I think."

He smiled, "Yeah, that's it, man. Five."

He went back to his drums and the band played some country numbers which weren't bad, but I never could get too excited about country music. Sometimes the melody's OK, but the rhythm's too dumb.

We used to hear country music once in a while on our radio, in The Bronx, when we were in high school. On WWVA, from Wheeling, West Virginia. We would try to get as many faraway stations as we could at night, and we would write them down on this list that we kept. It was the closest thing to traveling, I guess. Jack and I would stay up listening to music as late as we could. We were afraid to go to sleep, because once we did the music would stop and the next thing we knew it would be morning and time to spend another day in boring school.

But I never could listen to country music for very long. I would always picture this slick congressman from Nebraska wearing these fake country clothes with the string tie his assistant had bought for him that afternoon, dancing to it and smiling, and saying, "Hello, Martha. How's the little girl?" to a woman dancing near him whose name was Mary and who had a little boy.

So when this mean looking Chicano dude named Roberto, who was wearing a complete Fidel Castro suit, began to shout, "Rock and Roll!" and the band swung into some old hits like "Long Tall Sally," and Johnny Winter's version of "Rock and Roll Hootchie Koo," I wasn't sorry.

This Roberto was totally spaced out on a psychedelic. Apparently he was a friend of Nectarine's brother Angie the Janitor. Angie was in Chicago, but Roberto had come up from San Francisco for the wedding. He seemed to know he was at a party but I doubt that he knew what town or state it was in.

Just as he came over to me, as the band finished the set, the front door opened and these four Zohars came in carrying this huge wedding cake on this kind of stretcher they had constructed. From the way they were struggling with it, it must have been pretty heavy. They set it down in the corner to the left of the door and everyone began to sit on the floor facing the cake, leaving an aisle that led up to it.

Well, I wasn't sure what was going on, but when Roberto sat down, I sat down on the floor next to him. Then Myron and the boys began to play Mendelssohn's "Wedding March" in country rhythm, which I wouldn't have believed possible until I heard it, and up the aisle walks my brother wearing this red, white, and blue Uncle Sam suit that I later learned Nectarine had sewn for him, using her mother's huge American flag. Only, instead of the Uncle Sam hat, he had on this giant Mad Hatter's hat, that was kind of like Uncle Sam's stovepipe, but it was narrow at the base and got wider as it approached the top and was a little askew in the way it was structured. It was gold, and dotted all over with sparkling sequins. (The next day, Wheeler told me that when Jack realized Nectarine was cutting up the flag to make him a suit, he was visibly startled. But he quickly concealed his surprise and went along with it, and Nectarine didn't notice.)

Then Nectarine walked up the aisle wearing this white satin and lace wedding gown that looked like it had come across with Grandma Franklin on the old Oregon Trail. It was shiny and worn and yellowed in places like it had been ironed too many times. Beneath it, she wore these high old-fashioned boots that reached almost to her knees.

And, yes, she certainly did look lovely, with a string of fresh spring jonquils woven into the plaits of her soft blonde hair, pulled back in a ponytail for the evening, and her eyes sparkling, and this soft-straw hat on her head, covered with fresh fruit—apples and bananas and cherries—that she had somehow attached to it around the top of the brim.

And then, shyly behind her, followed little Lord Krishna with, yes, his skin dyed blue, carrying a pink satin pillow with the big Tom Mix secret-compartment ring that my brother had sent for in 1949 and had kept with him at all times since.

They approached the cake together, bride and groom, and stood facing it, and just as I wondered where "the preacher" was, there was this kind of explosion and up popped this skinny bearded guy, with glasses, from out of the cake. He was about forty years old and was beginning to bald.

He looked like the kind of guy who, back on the block, wouldn't have gotten picked in the choose-up for a stickball game, but who would have always gotten to play by having enough smarts to bring the ball.

Well, the trick didn't exactly come off, because the guy got icing on his glasses and in his beard, and we had to stop the wedding for a while so Becky could get a towel because the guy began to cry when some of the icing got into his eyes.

Roberto, the brown-beret type dude sitting next to me, was crying too, which surprised me because I could see him blowing up a branch of the Bank of America, but I couldn't picture him as the kind of guy who cried at a wedding. But he kept crying.

While the preacher was getting de-iced, I turned to Wheeler sitting behind me. "Hey, is this guy a real preacher?"

Wheeler laughed that crazy laugh of his that is permitted to only those few sane people who can groove on the madness of the world (and, sometimes, maybe even encourage it) and

he said, "*He* thinks so ."
"Does the state think so?"
"The state of California or the state of Opteema?"
"That's what I figured."
"OK, we're here for this here wedding," the preacher said, as I turned back toward him, "so in accordance with the wishes of the bride and groom who don't believe in words because, on the Planet Opteema, everyone knows from birth what that great visitor from Opteema to Pesseema, Lao-Tse, said, 'Those that know, don't speak, those that speak, don't know,' I'll keep the gab to a minimum."

("Oh, God," I thought, "Jack is beginning to get people on his trip. The train is beginning to pick up speed.")

"So I'll just ask the bride, as a formality, are you married already to someone else?"

"I don't know."

"*You don't know?*"

"Well, no, man . . . I mean, we were going to get married in New York when I told my old man, Moholy-Nagy, that I was pregnant . . . but I don't know . . . You see, we started to the city hall but we took this acid that morning and we had these bottles of champagne, and I'm not sure really what happened. All I know is that I never saw my old man again, and when I woke up the next morning, I was in this big sleeping bag with this black dude in Central Park."

"Well . . . ," the preacher said, "I don't know what to say . . . I mean, we want this first wedding on Earth of two Opteemans to go off OK, but I'd like a legal opinion on this."

He turned toward Wheeler who had had quite a bit of drugs and champagne on his own already, and was drinking most of a bottle of champagne without a glass at that very moment. Wheeler tried to stand, but he was a little wobbly, so he sat back down, saying, "Well, of course, we got common law as well as statutory law to consider here, and legal precedents both English and American, but it's my opinion, professionally speaking, of course, that, well, to tell the truth, all I can say is I hired a band and I got these Buddhists here to cater this affair, and everyone's here for a wedding, so I'd say it's my legal opinion that you just better marry these two fuckers or I'll come up there and put you back into the fuckin' cake."

Everyone began to cheer and applaud and Roberto jumped up and yelled, "That's no shit, man, cause I'll help."

Well, I guess the look on Roberto's face was the clincher, because the space-rabbi said, "Well, on the Planet Opteema, as we say from birth, 'Who gives a shit, anyways?'" and everyone began to shout "Yeah!" and "All *Right!*" and the spirits picked up, and Roberto sat back down, and he said angrily to me (tears still in his eyes from his crying), "That's no shit, man," and I patted him on the back and said, "Right on, brother," to calm him down, and the preacher said "OK," and he turned to Jack and he said, "Are *you* married?"

"No," Jack said. Then he turned to us and he said, "I was married once, but I got divorced. My wife and I would always fight. Neither of us could stand the other's religion. We were both Mormons."

Well, that got things back on an even keel, as a joke often will, and it got Jack to where he forgot about the wedding and went into a series of "wife-jokes"—"I mean, let me tell you about my first wife. Once I had my boss over for dinner and my wife . . . well, how can *anyone* make chicken-noodle soup and forget to put in the chicken? I mean, really! And then, after the meal was over . . . well, *really*, I mean how can anyone *burn* the tea. I mean seriously . . ."

Jack seemed prepared to go on all night, but the rabbi interrupted him and got him back down to Opteema, and said, "OK. I now, by the authority vested in me by those present, pronounce you Old Man and Old Lady."

And Jack took the Tom Mix ring from Jimi's pillow and placed it on Nectarine's finger and lifted up the brim of her hat with the fruit on it and kissed her, and the band hit the first chords of Jimi Hendrix's "Foxy Lady," and everyone leaped up and began to boogie and Nectarine jumped down and unlaced her boots and then jumped back up and began to dance barefoot with her Uncle Sam old man, still wearing his mad hat, and we all danced around them, even Roberto (who was still crying), and it was carnival in Rio as Wheeler turned on his light machines and Opteema swept over us like a giant seductive wave, pulling us back into itself in the powerful undertow of the rainbow light and the alluring music and the champagne and the dope.

And we danced madly together while this kind of family—the four Zohars who had carried in the cake, and several women and all these long-haired boys and girls, the whole family nude now—began to circulate among us with trays of joints and these weird hors d'oeuvres. Some of the kids couldn't have been more than ten or eleven years old, and they all were smoking dope, and I danced up to Wheeler and I shouted, "Who *are* these people?" and he shouted back, again with that crazy laugh of his, "They're the caterers."

"The caterers?"

"Yeah. They're called The Neo-Buddhist-Nudist Navajo Commune. I hired them."

"They look like Stoned Family Robinson," I shouted back at him.

"They're on their way to L.A. They got thrown off their land by the sheriff."

"How come?"

"The county said their teepees violated the building code."

The band hit the last chord of the song. Wheeler quickly, and unsteadily, made his way to the microphone, and announced, "Now, listen up, everybody, I've got these Buddhist caterers here, wandering around with hors d'oeuvres, and I want you all to eat and enjoy yourself, that's what they're here for, but at the same time, I just want everyone to know that I counted these Buddhists when they came in. There are fifteen of them. And I'm gonna make damn sure that when we finish up here there are still fifteen of them. I don't want anyone making off with one of my Buddhists. So enjoy them. Use them while you're here. But please, don't try to take one home."

It all seemed part of the dance.

Even Roberto, who was still following me around , crying. I took him by the shoulder and led him outside into the cool night air.

"Hey, man, the wedding's over. Why are you still crying?"

He wouldn't look me in the eye. "If only I had knowed," he mumbled. "If only I had knowed you was Angelo's brother-in-law," he began to cry more forcefully, "I never woulda took it."

"Took what?"
"Your overcoat."
"*What?* I don't have an overcoat."
"Last year. At Winterland. I never woulda stole your coat."
"I've never been to Winterland. I just got out here."
"How could I have stole Angelo's brother's coat?" he sobbed. "Angelo's *brother*." He stuck his chin out toward me. "Hit me, man."
"What?"
"Knock me out."
"But . . . I don't want to hit you."
"Come on, man. Hit me. I never shoulda done it."

Well, I couldn't reason with him, so I left him there with his chin out, and I went back in to the party, and took a stuffed cabbage that Becky offered me on a tray, and put it on one of the little plates that were stacked on the tray.

"I made these for the non-Buddhist-Nudists," she said.

I bit into it and it tasted better than the weird stuff to me, so I took another one, and Becky said, "I'll be out with the chopped liver in a little while," and I said to her, "Did you hear that surgeons in Israel have performed the first chopped liver transplant?" and she laughed as she moved through the dancers, offering her stuffed cabbage to all those who were still on the same planet she was, and I turned and there was Roberto, still wet-eyed, behind me.

So I offered him a bite of my stuffed cabbage (warm food or drink, as any army medic knows, is the best way to bring a shell-shock victim down), but he closed his mouth tight like a baby in a tantrum and pointed at his jaw. When I didn't punch him, he reached out with his right hand, grabbed the stuffed cabbage from the plate, and squashed it into his face. Well, by this time I had to face the fact that I wasn't going to convince him that he hadn't stolen my overcoat, so I wasn't sorry when he went into the bathroom and didn't come out.

Until I got worried and we had to break the door in (Becky had two locks on it). When we found him safely out cold in the bathtub, with tomato sauce from the cabbage still on his face, I was kind of relieved.

(The next afternoon, when I awoke, he was gone and I never saw him again.)

Chapter 15

AND SO WE DANCED the night away to sweet music and song, and when the sun awoke in the east, throwing our little party into dark relief, none of us was the happier for seeing it, because it meant the end of our joy-filled night.

When the band began to pack up, Jack announced that we were all to follow him in a marriage procession back to our new house. We picked up discarded jackets and crumpled sweaters. Nectarine looked for her boots. The band said goodnight and left. Jack went over to where Hark was lying on a rug next to Jimi and Shoshanna who had stayed awake as long as they could and then had crashed there in the corner and Hark had stretched out between them and the dancers as if to protect them from the feet of the stoned revelers. Jack took Hark by the front paws and began to waltz him around in the silence, the last couple on the floor, as we gathered ourselves together to follow him out into whatever it was he had planned.

"Where are my boots?" Nectarine demanded.

And it was true, they were nowhere in sight.

"To the woman who wears shoes, the whole Earth is covered with leather," Jack said, half-joking, as he joined the search.

"Fuck that," Nectarine said. "I want my boots."

Well, we looked and looked, but we couldn't even locate

one of them.

"They'll turn up, I'm certain of it," I said.

"Yeah, sure," Nectarine said. "Where the fuck is that 'Stoned Family Robinson'? The caterers. I'll bet those fuckers took them when they left."

"No, they couldn't have," Wheeler said slyly. "They're Buddhists."

"Maybe they're *Boot*ists," Nectarine said, and when we all laughed, sleepy-eyed and wearily, even she had to join in, although she tried not to, saying, "Well, I was *attached* to those boots." And as she put on her hat with the fruit on it, "Just like I'm attached to this hat."

"Then you should give up the hat, too," Jack said, this time completely serious. "The Buddha said attachments are the root of sorrow."

He got off his knees from where he'd been looking for the boots under Wheeler's big modern couch. Well, I expected Nectarine to give him a Chicago style, hog-butcher-to-a-nation "Fuck that, too," but I was surprised to find that he had hooked her and she only responded with a thoughtful, "Well, maybe so," as she concentrated on fixing her hat on her head.

"Sure," Jack said, more lively now. "Let's go over to God's little acre and perform the final ceremony of the night."

And I never found out whether he had planned the ceremony all along, or whether, in Opteema fashion, he had simply trusted in the fertility of circumstances to provide him with one when he needed it.

He led us in a double-file procession over to our acre, through the open gate, and around the house to the twenty-foot flagpole that was set in a concrete base about ten yards down the slope. And he lined us up in a semicircle between the house and the flagpole, facing down the hill toward the east. There was a long moment of silence as we drowned in the beauty of the morning together, good people, after a night of shared openness, now watching the sleep-heavy sun slowly crane itself over the white mist that hung over the snaky creek bottom like a thick ribbon.

And then, as we stood in the crisp quiet, Jack took Nectarine's hand and moved her out of the semicircle and down to the flagpole and, each facing the other, he looking to the south, she to the north, each in profile against the so slowly lifting sun, he kissed her gently on the lips and then he, gently, removed her fruit-full hat from her head, releasing her hair which she pulled out of its ponytail and shook out full in the gold morning light, and he pierced the rim of the hat with the steel catch fixed to the flagpole cord, and slowly, in the clean April light of the swollen sun, above the impossibly green, northwest-America grass, he raised the hat up smoothly until it came to rest beneath the small golden globe at the tip of the pole.

"I hereby name this land Opteema," he said, in a surprisingly soft, and even modest, voice. "This hat shall be our standard. And this pole, the . . . er . . . the . . . the Carmen Miranda Memorial Flagpole, shall be our staff."

He turned to Nectarine and waited, as if asking her benediction for the act of taking her hat, and she gave it to him with a smile that unfroze the weary lines in her face, and she leaned forward and gave her lips to him with a soft kiss, and then gave her body to him, moving against him, into his arms.

Chapter
16

NOW MAYBE I'M OVERLY SENSITIVE, but I can tell when I put my pants on whether or not the wallet's in the pocket. The next afternoon, when I woke up and got dressed, it wasn't.

That meant that my esteemed brother was out somewhere in the world, passing himself off as me, and making a purchase. Most likely of some goods that he felt would help make his dreams a reality.

I hadn't had more than twenty bucks in the wallet. I never carry much cash. That's why I never get robbed. So I was relieved to think that if he bought anything expensive, he'd have to Master Charge it. At least he'd have to shop in a regular store. Or so I thought.

Until I went upstairs and looked out the window and saw him walking up the road leading a big old horse. It was colored like a gutter in The Bronx in March—kind of slushy, with blotches of black.

As I rushed to the door to meet him, I passed Nectarine, in the kitchen, talking on the phone. (" . . . *her own kid!* Are you *kidding* me? How can you fuck a four-year-old kid? . . . ") I met Jack at the front gate.

"How can you Master Charge an old horse?" I shouted at him.

"Don't ask. It wasn't easy."

"How much was the damage?"

"A hundred and fifty bucks."

"My savings are almost gone. How're we going to live?"

"Don't worry. I got a line on a teaching job at the local junior college through this shrink Freudenberg that Wheeler knows."

Nectarine appeared on the porch behind me, along with Jimi and Hark. Hark began to bark at the horse but Jack silenced him.

"Wow! A horse! Far out!" Nectarine said. "Hey, Jimi, look at the horse."

"It's not for us," Jack said. "It's for Grandma Franklin."

He walked past the gate, leading the horse over to grandma's property. We followed.

"Grandma Franklin can't ride a horse," I said. "She can hardly walk."

"It's not for *her*, man. Just watch. But be quiet. I want it to be a surprise."

Well, we did watch. He took the horse to the front end of Grandma Franklin's mobile home, in the high grass and weeds, and we saw that he had attached a harness from an old wagon to the trailer hitch. He backed the big old horse into the harness, hooked him up, said, "Now just wait a minute here," and went into the mobile home.

When he came out, he was carrying Grandma Franklin piggyback.

"Surprise!" he shouted.

Grandma's face lit up like a TV. "Why, Jack . . ."

"It's for you, grandma. We bought it for you."

She beamed. "Why . . . it's just like when we came across the plains from Arkansas."

"I knew you'd like it," Jack said.

"It makes me feel like I'm on the move again."

"That's right, grandma," Jack said, carrying her up to the horse so she could pat its nose. "When you're tired of TV, you just look out the window and when the wind blows the high grass, you're on the road, kid."

Well, grandma was so delighted, I couldn't bring myself to think about the money it had cost. So I just asked Jimi if he wanted to sit on the horse, but fortunately he hid behind Nectarine. I say "fortunately," because I wasn't all that interested in getting near the old nag myself.

Jack carried grandma back into her mobile home.

"Horses don't bite," Nectarine said to me.

"Oh, yeah? Then how come they have teeth?"

We heard Becky laugh, as she came up the road toward us with Shoshanna. "He's right," Becky said. "If it can eat, it can bite."

I explained the wherewithal of the purchase to her.

"And you call yourself an accountant?" she said, still smiling.

"Even an accountant's got a heart," I said.

She patted me on the shoulder. "Here's Shoshanna," she said to Nectarine. "I've got to get over to the Center for an hour. We're having a talk on meditation by Swami Vishnu-Ananda. You might have heard of him. The first flying swami? He was on TV in his piper cub."

She walked away down the road, turning back once to look at the horse, as if she expected it to have disappeared.

"She really helps out at the Jewish Center?" I said.

Jimi peeped out at me from behind Nectarine's full skirt.

"Of course," Nectarine said, wondering why I would doubt it.

Jack came out of the mobile home without grandma on his back, and we headed over to our house. We walked through the open gate and sat on the porch steps.

"Mama, I wanna horse," Jimi said.

"I got you a dog," Nectarine said, pointing to Hark.

"I wanna *horse*."

"Here, take a pig," she said, moving off the steps to pick up four-fifths of a plaster piggy-bank from the debris of old, paint-chipped, maimed toys on the porch floor.

"Mommy, I want a *horse*."

"I gave you a pig. I don't have a goddamned horse," Nectarine said.

"Maybe he'll take a giraffe," Shoshanna said.

"I wanna 'raffe."

"I don't *have* a giraffe," Nectarine said.

"How about if I do some giraffe imitations?" I said.

"I have a giraffe at my house," Shoshanna said.

"OK. We'll go over there in a minute. You guys ever get

into meditation much?" Nectarine said, slowly lifting herself up to lead the giraffe hunt.

"What's that?" I said.

"Meditation?"

"No, that kind of moaning. Listen. It's like it comes from across the road."

"Yeah," Jack said. "I hear it, too. It's weird."

"Oh. That's Millicent's father." Nectarine dusted off the seat of her torn dungarees. "Millicent lives in that old house across the way. Her father's around two hundred years old. She takes care of him. He always moans like that. He's an invalid. I've never seen him." She reached down and took Jimi and Shoshanna by the hands and led them down the steps. "I don't even hear it anymore. She's a drag, Millicent. I don't talk to her."

"If she takes care of her father, she must be OK," Jack said. "I mean if this is going to be Opteema, we've got to see to that side of it."

"Well, suit yourself," Nectarine said. "But she's still a drag to me."

She led the kids through the gate. She turned, and said, "You guys were into a lot of meditation back east?"

"Nah," Jack said.

"The Vietnam war was his meditation," I said.

"Let's not get into *that*, now," Jack said, quickly.

"How about you?" she said to me.

"Well, I went to a Zen center for a while. But I didn't like it. No one told any jokes."

Nectarine laughed. "I know what you mean." She started off down the road with the kids. Then she said, over her shoulder, "Meditation to me is when you smoke dope with your legs crossed," and she walked off, cackling that wicked laugh of hers.

Jack and I sat there silently for a while, warm in the afternoon sun which filtered through the big Douglas fir that was rooted next to the porch.

"You say you might get a job?"

"Yeah. The guy who teaches the fiction writing class at the J.C. got cancer . . . It might be a lucky break for us.

"Us?"

"Sure . . . I know you're worried about the money situation. I bet you've even thought about getting a job."

"Well . . . "

"Well, you haven't had a vacation in two years. Take it easy. Do some writing if you have to keep busy. I know we spent almost all of your ten thousand bucks already . . . "

"That's OK. I like it here . . . "

"Sure. You've got to be on Opteema, too. That's the whole point. That's why I need this teaching job."

He picked up the piggy bank. Smiled as he looked into it through where the ass was broken off.

"That won't hold much money," I said.

"No, I guess not . . . You know, teaching would be the real test . . . An average group of people, from the most mellow section of the U.S. If I couldn't get them on Opteema . . . "

"A lot of people around here seem to be there already."

"Yeah. The freaks. But if we can't change the majority hallucination, that's what we'll be for our whole lives— freaks . . . That's why the teaching's so important. Everything depends on it."

"You know . . . nothing personal, but maybe you should dress up for the interview. The torn dungarees and the DeWitt Clinton High School football jersey are OK . . . they're great, in fact . . . but these people might want someone respectable."

"Like an accountant?" he smiled.

"My first husband was an accountant." She was crossing the road toward us. "Oh, I hope you boys don't think I'm intruding. I live across the way. My name is Millicent."

I didn't say so, but Millicent's first husband must have had a rough time with a wife like her because, as an accountant myself, I have to say she looked pretty ludicrous as she crossed the old country road over from her house. She was about fifty-five or sixty years old, thin and pale, wearing these high heels, and torn nylons, and an old, faded orange gown.

And her house wasn't exactly C.P.A. either. A kind of dirty, gray, broken-down shack, not far from the road. Some of the windows were these smokey kind of soft plastic sheets tacked onto the frames. They flapped in the breeze.

And her face was caked with make-up and rouge—like a

corpse at a funeral."

"I hear you boys bought the house."

"That's right," I said. "I'm Jerry. This is my brother, Jack. He just got married to Nectarine."

"Oh, yes. Laura Lee's daughter. Well, I don't care what anyone says about Nectarine, she's a lot nicer than her mother. Do you know Laura Lee is dating a jockey? No one around here liked her very well. Why, when she was younger, she even consorted with the apple pickers . . . if you know what I mean."

"She seemed OK to me," Jack said.

"Oh, er . . . well, of course. I understand your position. By the way, when you bought the house, did you check the maps at the title office?"

"We're having what they call a title search," I said.

"Of course. That's just to clear the title. That's OK. What I mean is, your house is so close to the road . . . well, it might have been built on county property. It might be on the road."

"The house is behind the fence," I said. "The road is on the other side."

"Yes, of course. But that's just the part of the road that was paved in 1931. Your fence might be on the *old* road. You see, your land goes all the way down to the creek. But Mrs. Franklin, I guess you've met her, Laura Lee's mother—well, like mother, like daughter, I always say—but, anyhow, you see, she built the house too close to the road . . . "

"Ommmm," Jack began to hum loudly, with his eyes closed.

"I told her she should have had it surveyed, but she wouldn't listen. ("Ommmm!"—louder) You boys didn't have it surveyed, did you?"

"No."

"OMMMMMMMMM!"

"Well, you ought to. Your house might be condemned."

When she said this, Jack increased the volume of his OMMMMMMMMMM until he sounded like one of those records of racing cars that guys get when they buy expensive stereos but they don't like music.

"Er . . . Your brother . . . is he all right?"

"Yes. It's his religion. He's a Zen Buddhist."

"Oh . . . I thought he looked Jewish."

"Well, he's part Jewish. But our mother was only half Jewish. And half Oriental."

"She was an Ori-yenta," Jack said.

"Oh . . . " She looked puzzled. When she saw Nectarine coming back along the road with the kids, Millicent said, "Well, I must go now. Father needs me. Just trying to be neighborly."

And she beat it back to her shack, almost falling twice in her driveway when her heels slipped on bits of gravel.

"On Opteema, we won't have people like that," Jack said.

"I know. But what do you do with them *here?*"

"OMMMMMM!"

That seemed to satisfy him. But it didn't help me much. We were in debt for 17 Gs on the house. I wondered what would happen if it got condemned. Maybe Millicent was right.

In the Big Apple we didn't have these kinds of problems that we were running into in the big apple orchard. You rented a place. And then you let the landlord worry about it.

And as bad as some landlords can be, at least you always had someone to blame when you were feeling miserable and low.

Chapter
17

"HEY, YOU GUYS, come on over here." Nectarine was standing with the kids beside a small tree that stood between our house and the road, on our side of the fence. We walked over to them.

"The ornamental plum tree is beginning to bloom," she said.

We were surprised to see these little pink flowers hatching out of the buds. Jack got all excited. "Oh, hey, great! You won't see a flowering plum tree on MacDougal Street. Hey, see, this country is all right," hitting me on the bicep.

"I didn't say it wasn't."

"Oh, man, it's great. It's natural, Jerr. The hell with Pesseema and its cities. This is *real*."

Back on the porch, we sat quietly, playing with the kids and their stuffed, toy giraffe. The light softened slightly as the sun began to get ready to close up shop and go home. Becky came up the road with Wheeler. He was still wearing his sport jacket and brown slacks. He had just returned from law school in The City. (North of San Francisco, everyone calls it The City.) They walked through the gate and sat on the steps with us. They each kissed Shoshanna. Wheeler gave her a big bear hug. Becky took her on her lap. She smoothed Shoshanna's hair. "Hey, were you guys thinking about getting a car?"

"Yeah," I said.

"Well, I might have something for you. This nice, kind of

spaced-out guy named Mel, whose younger brother goes to the Center, is selling an old VW. He said he'll be in tomorrow. I got his address."

"Great," I said. "We'll go see him. OK, Jack? What time's your interview?"

"One."

"We'll go in the morning."

"You guys should drop by the Center, sometime," Becky said. "I'll introduce you to the people there."

"Oh, no. Not me," I said. "When the next pogrom comes, I want to be as far from the Jewish Center as possible."

"No, really . . . , " she smiled.

"It's easy for you to be brave. When they start sacking the temple, you just go into, 'Old Man River' and they'll think you're the janitor."

"How about you, Jack? You're still Jewish. You can't fool me."

"I know I am. But I'm putting it into my writing."

"I thought you weren't going to write anymore," Nectarine said.

"I've decided to write The Great Jewish Novel. I'm calling it, 'The Brothers Karamatzo.'"

"No . . . I mean it," Becky said.

"It's true. You see, I have this theory about man that I feel stems from my Jewish roots. I believe man is a bagel."

"A *bagel?*" Wheeler said.

"Yeah . . . It's true. Man is basically a long hole with some matter around it . . . I mean it . . . "

"I can't talk straight to you guys," Becky laughed.

"They came to California, so they think that makes them Christian," Nectarine said.

"Don't forget, Christ was Jewish," Wheeler said.

"Even if he wasn't Jewish, his Father certainly was," Jack said.

"Well, look at Martin Luther," I said.

"What does that have to do with it?" Becky said.

"He was Lutheran," I said.

"Look at Mary Magdalene," Jack said. "Now I ask you, is that a Jewish name? *Magdalene?*"

"Well, look at Joseph of Arimathea," Wheeler said. "Is

that a Jewish name? *Arimathea?"*
"Look at Genghis Khan," Jack said.
"OK," I said, "that's Jewish. *Kahn.* There's no doubt about that at least."
"You guys are crazy," Becky said. "Nuts."
"Speaking of nuts," Wheeler said, "what are we going to do for dinner?"
"How about a pizza?" I said. "There's no sense anyone cooking on such a nice spring evening."
Everyone agreed. Wheeler went to get his van and we walked over to Grandma Franklin's. Jack carried her out piggyback and we all piled into the van and headed toward Santa Rosa, a small city seven miles east across the so-flat, Kansas-like basin, set against the foothills before Mount St. Helena.
On our way home it was already dark in the valley as we drove west toward the hills between our new home in Sebastopol and the sea. The kids were asleep and no one spoke in the van as we steeped in the silence of my favorite time of day. And the way the houses on our side of the hills had already climbed under the covers of night while the sky above them was still light with the last refracted rays of the gone sun made me think of that Magritte painting where the little house is in the dark, and the street light in front of it is lit, but when you look up you're startled to find that in the sky, it's still day.
Some of that "non-realistic" art is more real than it seems at first.
We said goodnight in Wheeler's driveway under a big full moon that rose over the hills in the east. It shone like the head of a bald junkie nodded out on the counter of Riker's at 3:00 A.M.
"You guys really should come over to the Center," Becky said, trying one last time. "You have to admit, a part of you is still Jewish."
"Of course we are," I said. And then I proclaimed to the star-sprinkled, clear night sky, "Are we not descended from Abraham, Isaac, and Newton?"
"You guys are out of your minds," Becky said.
"I certainly hope we are," Jack said.

We said one last series of goodnights. Jack picked up sleeping Jimi and carried him back to our house in his arms. I picked up Grandma Franklin on my back and carried her over to her mobile home.

Chapter 18

> Spring sunshine.
> Tiny plum tree buds open.
> All the time flowers inside.

THE NEXT MORNING, when I came upstairs from the room in the basement where I slept, I found that haiku on the blackboard nailed to the kitchen wall to the right of the stove. It made me feel good to read it. Maybe Jack would start to write again.

I passed Nectarine talking on the telephone (" . . . well, standing on your head isn't necessarily religious . . . ") and headed for the master bedroom to shake Jack out of his sleep.

But he wasn't there. I had suspected that my wallet felt a little lighter when I put my pants on. Sure enough, three singles were missing.

I found Jack in the backyard, with Hark and Jimi, at the flagpole. He had just finished attaching the fresh fruit to the hat.

"Look, Jack," I said, approaching him as he fixed the hat back onto the steel catch of the flagpole cord, "I don't mind paying for a symbol, but at least I want to know what it *means*."

"Please!" Jack said, in a kind of mock reverence, signaling me to put my hand over my heart. "Silence. The Carmen Miranda Memorial Flagpole ceremony is about to begin."

So I stood there, with my hand over my heart, Jimi standing next to me, imitating me, as Jack raised the hat up the flagpole. Then he began to sing "Cuanto Le Gusta" while dancing a little samba around the pole with Hark, as Jimi giggled with delight.

"We have no word for 'meaning' on the Planet Opteema," he

said, in answer to my question, as he led us back up to the house. "Let's get some breakfast and go look at that VW. I borrowed Becky's car."

Mel, the guy with the VW, lived on the other side of town. He was a gentle sort, about twenty-three, with longish, dirty-blond hair and a light-brown mustache. The car was parked in front of his house. It was rust colored, and this was fortunate, because most of the body was rusting.

Mel led us down across the lawn to the car. "It's pretty banged up, but it runs real good."

"I like a Volkswagen," Jack said. "My first wife had a bug. Once, she was driving along, when she sees this lady standing by another Volkswagen. The lady has the front hood open and she looks puzzled. So my wife stops alongside. 'Something the matter?' my wife said. 'The car wouldn't start, so I opened the hood, and look, someone's stolen the motor.' 'That's OK,' my wife says, 'I have an extra one in the back.'"

The guy looked puzzled. Country folks are nice, but they're not always right there on the uptake, if you know what I mean.

"Why don't you listen to how it sounds?" Mel says.

"Sure," Jack says, and he gets Hark and Jimi in the back, and then he gets in the driver's seat and turns on the radio, listens for a minute, and says, "It sounds fine."

"I meant the engine."

"What do I know about engines? Radios I know . . ."

"Well, why don't you take her out for a spin?"

"Take Rusty?" Jack says.

"Rusty?"

"Yeah. The car."

"Her name isn't Rusty," Mel says.

"Of course it is," Jack says. "Just look at her. It's obvious. How long you had this car?"

"Three years."

"Well, at least by now you should know her name."

Mel breaks into a goofy smile. "Anyhow, she sure runs good." He hands Jack the keys. "Take her out for a drive. I'll be here for another half hour or so. If I'm not, just leave her in front of the house. The registration's in the glove compartment."

And he walks into his house!

Well, when I saw Willie Mays make that back-to-the-plate catch on Vic Wertz in the '54 series, I thought I had seen everything, but this took the cake.

I mean, can you imagine going to buy a car from a guy in The Bronx, and he gives you—a perfect stranger—the keys and registration, and he says, "Take her out for a drive. If I'm not here when you get back, just leave her in front of the house."

Let's face it, it's just not possible. A guy like that in The Bronx could never make it to the age where he could get a license. He'd be Darwinned-out before he was twelve.

Anyhow, we just took a drive for fifteen minutes since neither of us knew the first thing about cars except they run or they don't, and this one did. So Jack decided to buy it.

"Shouldn't we take a look at some others?" I said.

"Are you kidding? Rusty is part of the dream. She's our official car. Just *look* at her . . . Besides," he smiled, "I need her to get to my interview this afternoon. I've got to get Becky's car back by twelve-thirty."

Well, I did take another look at her. With all the interior lining gone from the ceiling and the doors. The seat springs right there, coiled where the cushions used to be. One window broken and the window on the driver's side missing.

But the radio played. And the engine worked. And somehow it did seem an appropriate car for us to have at the time. So I wrote Mel a check for Rusty. But when I handed it to him, you can bet I didn't offer to show him any I.D. I figured it might offend him in some weird way.

We piled in and chugged back to Opteema. Jack and Hark and Jimi and me, in our new "official car." You know, there's one thing about being nuts—or at least about being in a special kind of nuts space—while you're there, everything seems to be fitting together real fine.

It's like being in the army. You can never afford to see how truly crazy it is until you're on the outside again.

When we got back to Becky's house, we realized we had left her car at Mel's.

Chapter
19

WHILE I WAS WAITING for Jack to come back from his interview, Wheeler came by, straight from school, to offer me a job. I could work for him, on weekends, starting in June, at a flea market in a place called Alameda, over near Oakland. Selling car tapes or something. Just two days a week, and a few hours to do the books, and I'd still have the month of May off. I didn't have time to get all the details (he had to run to meet Becky) but I accepted on the spot. Wheeler paid a decent wage, and the hours were just what I wanted.

Nectarine was trying to drown some gophers in her garden. We put the hose down the gopher holes and let fly, hoping to flood them out. Although we tried for over an hour, I didn't see any gophers, but Nectarine was convinced it would work.

All this time I was thinking about Jack. I had told him not to take a Great Dane to a job interview, but try to tell someone like Jack anything.

And the way he looked—he usually wore these "bum clothes"—shiny pants or patched dungarees, his football jersey or a worn work shirt, and torn sneakers—so I was relieved when we got back from Mel's the second time and he told us he was going to dress up.

A half hour later, out he pops for Nectarine and me to inspect him. And he's smiling away, pleased as punch, in his sport jacket from the Goodwill, his "good" pants which were even shinier than his "bum" pants, and these old black shoes he's had since college. They looked like priest's shoes. I don't know, maybe he felt safe from Irish gangs in them, but they just didn't make it with anyone else.

I didn't have the heart to tell him.

"How do I look? I didn't want to look like a bum, so I dressed up."

"Er . . . fine. Just fine."

"Nectarine?"

"You look like a bum who dressed up."

Good old Nectarine. The Queen of Tact. But Jack just laughed and went off to his interview. And, to tell you the truth, he did look pretty confident and together, in a seedy, novelist kind of way.

Anyhow, he came back smiling.

"Did you get it?" Nectarine and I both said.

He just kept smiling. Jimi jumped over the hose and ran up to him, and Jack picked him up and swung him around in the air.

"Jack?" Nectarine said.

"Please . . . ," he said. "First, the ceremony."

So while we're waiting in the garden for the news—Nectarine leaning on her hoe, me still flooding Gopher City with a volume of water that must've driven their weathermen bananas—Jack goes over to the flagpole, salutes with his hand over his heart, lowers and removes the hat, does an abbreviated samba once around the pole with Hark to a few bars of "Cuanto Le Gusta," and then turns to us, smiles and says, "I got it."

"Jack!" Nectarine says, and rushes up to hug him. I hug him, too.

"You didn't take Hark in then," I say.

"Sure I did. It was in this classroom. I just had him lie down next to me. There were about seven people there questioning me . . . You'd be surprised how many people want to be your friend when you've got a giant dog with you."

He began to walk toward the house, Jimi on his shoulders, the sacred hat in his hand. Nectarine and I followed.

"This junior college is great, man. I had a good omen on

the way over in Rusty. I found this kind of spaced-out guy wandering on the mall of the freeway. So I picked him up. I could hardly understand what he was saying, but I took him to the school. When I let him off in the parking lot, he gave me a dime. Can you dig it? This spaced-out student gave me me a *tip!* He thought I was a taxi driver." Jack laughed. "Oh, man, when that happened, I knew I was in."

"When do you start?" Nectarine said, as I walked over to the spigot and decreed clear skies and fair weather for Gopherland for the evening.

"In June. This dude Chavers, that got sick, was scheduled for a summer course. So I have that one, and then one in the fall."

As we got to the front steps, Millicent saw us from across the road and called to us. She walked toward us, hesitated for a second when she saw Nectarine, but then came up to the fence anyways. She was wearing the same gown, but this time she had on this strange, orange, wide-brimmed hat with a veil, and she was carrying an orange and white cat.

"I didn't want to bother you boys, but there's something I had to tell you."

"Oh yeah?" Jack said.

"That's right. You know, there's been talk about their building a highway here, along this street, and I thought you might want to look into it, because if they do, what with your house being so close to the road, your house would probably be condemned, and . . ."

"Yeah, OK," Jack interrupted her. "We'll check it out."

"Yes, well, that's all I had to tell you. To be forewarned is to be forearmed, my late husband used to say."

"Well, it's better to be four-armed than to be four-eyed," Jack said.

But she ignored him. "Did you hear about that aluminum heiress those black men kidnapped? She doesn't want to come home."

"If I were made of aluminum, I wouldn't want to come home either," I said.

"No, she's not *made* of aluminum," Millicent giggled, "She's heir to the aluminum money."

"Aluminum money?" I said. "Who ever heard of aluminum

money?"

"Well, anyhow," Millicent said, "I think it's terrible. Just terrible. Those black men must have brainwashed her."

"Maybe they just gave her a good fuck," Nectarine said.

Millicent began to stutter and sputter. Just then, "Old Faithful," her father, let out one of his hourly moans from inside her house.

"The *memento mori*," Jack said.

"What?" Millicent said, sensing some secret Yiddish insult.

"Your father," I explained. "Jack says he's moaning."

"Oh, yes. He misses me so, when I go out."

And she plopped over the pebbles in her heels, toward her wreck of a house, which we now called "The Cat House," since Nectarine had told us she had twelve cats inside. When the wind came over from the west in the evening, I knew Nectarine wasn't kidding. It was a mixture of fresh, oxygenated, salt air from five thousand miles of clean Pacific space, and cat piss from across the street.

At least in New York, *everything* stinks so bad your nose goes out of business after a few years and you don't have to smell anything at all.

We went into the house. Jack left the fruit on the hat and placed the entire holiness on the bottom shelf of the refrigerator. He grabbed a couple cans of Oly and we sat down at the kitchen table with Nectarine who was spooning out some yogurt to Jimi.

"I can't believe your good luck, Jack," I said. "And mine, too."

I told him about Wheeler's job offer.

"I'm telling you, this is *It*," Jack said. "It's just a question of opening your eyes. You know what I did on the interview? I walked in there with a dictionary in my hand. And before they could even ask me a question, I set fire to it. Right there in front of them."

"You didn't!" I exclaimed.

Nectarine cackled her wicked laugh.

"Yes, I did. I figured if they're going to test me, I'm going to test them. I'm not teaching in Pesseema U. That game is over."

"What happened then?"

"I slammed the dictionary closed and put out the fire. They pretty much ignored it. Then this nice old guy asked me about the symbolism of what I had done. So I told them I was done with writing, forever."

"And they accepted that?"

"Well, I guess they seemed to think I was kidding. They all began to tell me how much their students had liked my book, and how glad they were to meet me. Finally, I interrupted them and I said, 'I'm serious about not writing. Words are leaks.'"

"You're kidding. You didn't say that . . ."

He laughed. "I told them that in the beginning was the Word, and the Word was God, and that I had enough of God by the time I was twelve—he reminded me too much of my father. Well, I was serious, but they just cracked up."

"Far out!" Nectarine said.

"Far ow!" Jimi said.

Jack laughed, nibbled on Jimi's hair, took a drink of beer, and continued, "I even told them that the snake in the Garden of Eden was Adam's tongue."

"And they *hired* you?"

"That's right. Absolutely," he said, proudly. "Summer and fall. They said it was the most interesting job interview they'd given in a long time. They were terrific. Wonderful folks."

"I don't understand it around here."

"You've got to loosen up, that's all," Nectarine said, smoking her evening joint. "If you bring all those Pesseema vibes with you, people respond to where you're at." She wiped Jimi's mouth with the end of the tablecloth she had crocheted. "You get the world you expect."

"Well . . . I don't know . . ."

And I didn't.

This California wasn't what I had expected. I had to admit it. I knew how to write a corporate budget, and how to make up an organization chart, by function, by product, or by geographical area, but nothing I had learned in business school had taught me how to deal with this weird kind of shit.

Chapter
20

THE NEXT TWENTY OR THIRTY DAYS were very pleasant. But I'll tell you the truth, it wasn't all jokes and lying around and games. Sometimes we couldn't think of any jokes. Then it was just lying around and games.

The nights were another story. I didn't sleep well in the basement. My room itself was pleasant enough, except for the fact that the ceiling and I were the same height.

I even had a window on the backyard, facing an old apricot tree. (Because of the slope of the land, the house was one story in front, two in back.) I wish I could say I lay on my bed in the peaceful country night and listened to the train's plaintive whistle, sounding in the distance like the moo of a hollow iron cow. But the night sounds bothered me. Strange buzzings and flappings and scurryings and occasional weird howlings in the dark.

And every week or so, I would hear Jack upstairs suddenly scream and thrash about during one of those nightmares that had been invading him since we left Nam. These dreams of his shook me up too. Because I knew what they were like. I'd had a couple myself.

But it was Old Faithful I listened to most. Every hour on the hour. Wailing out his terminal loneliness in solitary dotage, surrounded by a crazy daughter and twelve pissing cats.

It gave me the chills.

Nectarine was used to it, but I knew this Pesseeman lament was not escaping the ears of my brother. Even though he never spoke about it.

Nectarine noticed that I wasn't sleeping well and she invited me to move upstairs. I said it was just bad dreams. When she insisted on knowing what they were about, I told her I had a recurring nightmare in which I was being bitten by a Ninevite.

It was during this period that Jack began to neglect to hitch up Jeff for Grandma Franklin. Sometimes I would go over and fill in for him. And I hate to admit it, but after I got to know him, I began to like the beast.

Jack had taken to staying inside the house almost all day, wearing this blue satin "smoking jacket" Nectarine had bought for him at the Salvation Army, and pretending he was Haydn's patron, Prince Esterhazy. Each afternoon, he would move the stereo speakers up to the back windows of the house, and while Nectarine played with the kids in the grass and I read under the apricot tree, he would play us some Haydn and Mozart.

He continued to perform the flagpole ceremony every morning and evening. And this didn't seem like such a crazy notion after a while. At least it got him out of the house twice a day. And every couple days he would join us in a walk to town so he could buy fruit for the hat at the Safeway. He liked to pick out the fresh fruit himself so he could be sure it was fresh.

I have to admit the people at the Safeway thought he was a little strange. It wasn't just the Prince Esterhazy suit, but also the old Buddhist prayer Jack had learned when he began to study Buddhism between flying helicopter missions in Nam:

I take refuge in the Buddha.
I take refuge in the Dharma. [The law; the Way.]
I take refuge in the Sangha. [The Buddhist Monastic Order.]

Each time Jack entered the Safeway, he would walk to a spot between the big plate glass windows and the middle check-out teller, he would kneel facing the tellers and the racks of food behind them, and he would recite slowly, in a loud, deep voice:

> I take refuge in the Buddha.
> I take refuge in the Dharma.
> I take refuge in the Safeway.

He would cross himself as he said each line.

Well, the people in town weren't narrow-minded by any means, but this kind of upset them. Gave them the willies, if you know what I mean.

Becky, our Sociologist-in-Residence (Jack had named her that), saw this in a second. So she hurried to introduce Jack to Joe Henderson, the manager.

The Safeway was a large, modern one, with the ceiling two floors high. The manager's office was up a flight of stairs behind the meat counter, over the back room where the butchers worked. If you think of the Safeway as a movie theater, then Joe Henderson's office was where the projection booth would be. From his large window, he could look out over the entire store.

Joe was a friend of Becky's and Wheeler's, a neat, nice man in his late thirties. When Becky told Joe that Jack was *her* friend, a New York novelist and a future professor at the local junior college, Jack got tenure in the store.

Since Joe realized there was no way to reason with Jack over his "religion," he just instructed the check-out tellers to announce to the folks who happened to be in line whenever Jack exorcised the store: "Nothing to worry about. He's a novelist from New York."

And it worked. Somehow it seemed to explain his behavior to the customers' satisfaction.

As for myself, though, I was still worried about him. Wheeler said Jack just needed an audience. He wasn't writing, but when he started teaching he would cheer up. I could see Wheeler's point, but I felt Jack needed a special kind of audience—one that was ready for his ideas about Opteema. I felt that it was because his writing audience had taken these ideas as "interesting fantasy" that he had turned to teaching.

I hoped the teaching would go better for him. I didn't see where else he could turn if it failed.

Chapter
21

"AND NOW, FOR YOUR LISTENING PLEASURE, I shall play Mozart's *Eine Kleine Nachtmusik*."

It was Jack. Inside the house. On an afternoon late in May. Perhaps a Tuesday. We'd lost track of the days. From where we stood in the garden, Nectarine, Jimi, Shoshanna, Hark, and me, we could barely make out his face behind the window screen.

During the third movement, Jack suddenly rejected the record.

"Prince?" I shouted up toward the house. "Everything OK?"

He didn't answer, but I saw him move past the window, all hunched over. I guess I haven't mentioned that one thing he did with his time was perfect his Quasimoto imitation. When he wasn't being Prince Esterhazy, dignified and refined, playing Mozart records and sometimes introducing one with an historical and musicological summary, he often ran around inside the house, hunched up, his face contorted, in his Quasimoto. Sometimes when we would go into the house for a drink of water or something, he would pop out of a doorway and try to scare us.

It was pretty hard to keep up with him and anticipate these sudden changes. Just when you'd be expecting the hunchback of Notre Dame, he'd appear as Prince Esterhazy and discuss eighteenth-century music in the most genteel manner.

On this particular day, after he ran around hunched for about ten minutes, he turned the stereo back on and blasted out a Count Basie LP. Then he came out of the house, walking regular again, with a banana in his hand. Hark ran up to him, carrying a rubber ball in his mouth.

"I thought you were Prince Esterhazy," I said.

"I was. Now I'm Count Basie."

"Count Basie is playing in New York. I saw it in the Voice yesterday."

"I know."

"Then how can you be Count Basie?"

"On Opteema, one of our basic laws is: The same thing can be in two places at the same time."

He reached down, took the ball from Hark's mouth, and threw it way down the hill toward the oak trees by the creek. Hark bounded after it.

"Do you know the Zen parable of the ship in the bottle?" he said. "The disciple comes up to the master and he says, 'Can you get a ship out of a bottle?' And the master concentrates for a second, and then he says, 'There! It's out.' You see? What he's saying is, if you can imagine a ship *in* a bottle, *I* can imagine a ship *out* of a bottle."

"And Count Basie?"

"Well, if you can imagine that there really is a Count Basie who comes from Red Bank, New Jersey, and that he's in a giant city called New York at this very moment, then I can believe that I *am* Count Basie."

"Well, if you're Count Basie, where's your band?" I said, quickly.

I thought I had him there for a moment, but then Nectarine chimed in with, "Look, man, things are tough enough around here without a fucking logician on the premises . . . It's just attachments, man. You can't let go. You're always protecting the majority hallucination."

Well, I let go of the argument and took the ball from Hark and threw it down the hill, pretending I was "Steady-Eddie" Lopat, the third best pitcher on the Yankees when I was a kid. Jimi and Shoshanna followed Jack over to the flagpole. He lowered the hat, looked it over from several angles, and then fastened the fresh banana to it in the "right place."

Of course I thought Nectarine was just oversimplifying things. But I have to admit that a part of me did wonder just what I *was* protecting. And why I should care to protect it.

I mean, if it made my brother happy to think he was Count Basie, what the hell did I care? Maybe it would turn out to be socially productive. He might go to the city and discover another Lester Young or something.

Maybe that's the way things like that happened.

But as I watched him carefully raising that crazy hat up the flagpole, I still wished I could be sure he was one hundred percent only *pretending* he was Count Basie.

I didn't say this. I figured Nectarine would answer that the whole notion of "pretending" was only another of my bourgeois hangups. And maybe she's right, I thought. After all, I am a bourgeois.

"You guys want to go to town?" Jack said. "I need another apple for my flagpole."

We all agreed to walk to the Safeway with him.

"Jack, just what is this business with the flagpole?" I said to him. "What's it really mean?"

"I don't know yet."

"Then why do you do it?"

"It just *feels* right. The same thing happens in writing. Some people think you invent your symbols to say what you mean. But you don't. That's backwards. They just come to you. And sometimes you just *know* that one is right. But you might not find out all it 'means' for years. You might even be lucky enough to keep getting meanings from it for the rest of your life."

We began to walk toward the house.

"Why don't you write anymore? You're such a good writer . . ."

He stopped walking and looked directly at me.

"Why don't *you* write, Jerr?"

"*Me?*"

"Yes, you . . . If you're so anxious to find out what this means, why don't you write a book about it? Call it, 'The Carmen Miranda Memorial Flagpole,' and write about what we're doing here, and see what happens . . . Because I'm not kidding when I say I'm not going to write anymore. My *life* is my novel now. If something feels right, I *do* it. I don't just write about it."

"Are you serious?"

"Why not?"

He began to walk up the hill again. I moved quickly to catch up to him.

"Will you help me?"

"Sure, Jerr." He smiled. "Just sign up for my course."

When we got inside the house, I called the J.C. to find out how to sign up for Jack's course.

Chapter 22

PRESIDENT MUGGED—ASSAILANT GETS TEN DOLLARS AND FLEES

JACK HAD CHANGED THE MESSAGE on Laura Lee's blackboard. Before we left for town, I turned to Jimi and I said, "You want to go to the Safeway?"
"No."
"Where do you want to go?"
"Supermarket."
"Oh . . ."
The Safeway was in "Greater Downtown Sebastopol," as Jack called the tiny shopping area of the town. It was about a half mile from our house.
As we passed through our gate and turned down the road, Millicent intercepted us. Jack was carrying a box of matzos. He had taken to doing this whenever he left the house.
"Isn't it a wonderful view behind your house," Millicent said. "It's certainly too bad they may put a development in on the slope behind the creek. That would really spoil it for you, I guess."
"Madam," Jack said, "nothing can spoil anything for us. If they put in a development, we'll just move somewhere else. I'm independently wealthy."
"Oh . . . ," Millicent said, impressed.
"I made a fortune in matzo futures in the thirties. I had F.D.R.'s ear. 'Jack,' he told me, 'buy matzo futures. Once we get into the war, and save the Jews, they'll be worth a pretty

penny.'"

"You're kidding," she said, in an uncertain tone.

"Here, try one."

He held the box out to her. She jumped back as if it contained a snake.

"They're good," Jack said, nibbling on one and offering one to me. "I really almost hit the jackpot back then," he said to Millicent. "If the world monetary system had collapsed, the matzo might have become the new international unit of exchange."

"Well, yes . . . ," Millicent said, backing off. "I just wanted to mention the development to you."

"To be forewarned is to be forearmed," Nectarine said.

"I wanna go supermarket," Jimi said.

Hark chased one of Millicent's cats up an apple tree.

Millicent turned back to us. "Well, it really doesn't matter anyway. The Russians and the Chinese will take over California in a couple years. Then no one will own anything anyway."

"I used to live in Russia," Jack said.

"Oh, really?" Millicent said.

"Yeah, but I had to leave. I kept getting arrested for having 'Dreams without Redeeming Social Significance.'"

Millicent's father moaned.

"I wonder if he heard my joke," Jack whispered to me.

"Well, I really must be getting home. My father needs me."

As Millicent walked across the road, Nectarine said, loudly, "Tell me, Jack, do you think the phallus is a guitar symbol?"

Millicent gave no sign of having heard.

"I don't know much about sexual symbolism," Jack said. "When I was in college, I wrote a thesis on 'The Clothed-Person in Western Art.'"

Hark left the cat up the tree and flopped down the road after us. We could walk along the center of the road because it dead-ended just beyond grandma's house, so hardly anyone ever used it.

"When you're writing, how do you find your material?"

"Once you start collecting it, Jerr, it becomes obvious. It's always happening, but no one except artists and some strong, sensitive people can afford to see it. The world's a lot more crazy than most people care to notice."

"Then how do you remember it all?"

"You just get a cheap ball-point pen and a little pad and you write it down as it happens."

We stopped for a minute, as Shoshanna took a pebble out of her shoe.

"I mean," Jack continued, "who would ever believe that a black woman from Harlem is an assistant to the social director of a synagogue in Sonoma County, California? But she *is*, damn it."

Around the almost right-angle bend, the road was blocked by a big van: SPCA.

"Uh, oh," Jack says, looking down at Hark who not only doesn't have a license, but doesn't even have a leash or collar. Jack moves up ahead of us quickly and gets Hark to heel. He leans toward Hark, arm stiff, fist closed, just like he had him on a leash. And, nonchalantly, he walks by the van in that position.

But it probably wasn't even necessary. The guy in the SPCA uniform was a soft-looking, bearded man about our age. As Jack passed, he came out of the neat, white house and over the astro-turf lawn carrying a little brown Pomeranian with a neat pink bow on its collar, followed by a sad-looking, middle-aged couple.

The woman had this cramped face—like she had tried to fit into God's suitcase and he had closed it on her head. Her husband was bald with an elongated head. God had caught him sideways.

They're each looking at the gravel on the side of the road or at the embarrassed SPCA guy, who's standing there holding the tiny dog awkwardly as if it were a turd. They won't look at each other.

Then the woman says, still looking down, "She slept with daddy for six months. Never bit nobody. Then he threw the hatchet at her. That's why she bit him."

He doesn't say a word. They just stand there. Silent and frozen. And up above, at the picture window, stands the woman's mother, in her dark blue dress and light blue hair. And she seems frozen, too. Like in a George Tooker painting.

Everyone looking like they once saw something that was too terrifying to remember. So now the dread that inhabits them has become nameless. And therefore more damaging.

We walked quickly past them. I couldn't say why, but the whole scene seemed to say, "Write me down. I stand for something you won't understand until later."

It spooked me. When we caught up to Jack, I looked into his eyes and I understood he had seen it all too. He nodded slightly to me. I felt much closer to him.

I was learning to see what he saw. I was learning to become a writer.

I was beginning to understand why writers go crazy.

We cut through the town park. On the grass, a woman in her thirties. By herself, on her knees, with these huge breasts rolling out over the top of her bikini. She's praying. No one seems to notice. But as we pass by her, Jack turns to me and gives me the slightest nod.

At the edge of the park, I run across the street and into the drugstore to buy a Bic pen and a pad.

We decide to stop at the library. Outside, we meet Becky who has brought four old people in a van. We all go inside together. The librarian, in her fifties, with rimless glasses and tight gray hair tied in a bun, sees Jack entering the sacred precinct with his box of matzos and his Great Dane. She doesn't know that his book is right there behind her on the shelf. She freaks.

"You can't come in here with *that!*"

"Madam, there is nothing wrong with matzos."

"Not *matzos!* The dog. Get him out of here!"

"Madam, please, this is not just a dog. This is Hark the Wonderdog. He is here to borrow some books by Albert Payson Terhune. We'll start with *Lad of Sunnybank*, if you don't mind."

"Get him *out* of here!"

"Oh, man, what a drag," Nectarine says, but she takes Hark and the kids outside.

"Is there something *you'd* like to see?" the woman says to Jack in an astringent tone.

"Yes. I want a particular German child-rearing book. But I don't suppose you'd have it in such a *small* library as this."

"We have more books than you think."
"Well, on second thought, you probably would have it."
"What's it called?"
"*Bringing Up Nazi.*"

Before she can answer, Jack stomps out, slamming the door behind him.

An old man, who had come with Becky, walks up to me. He has a gray, disheveled beard, hair to match, and thick glasses. He looks the way I imagine a Talmudic scholar would look, although I never met one in The Bronx.

"You know when it's Moses' birthday?" he says.
"No."
"The seventh of Adar."
"Oh, good. Now I'll be sure to send him a card."
He laughs.
"You see the *Ten Commandments?*" he says.
"No, I didn't."
I pretend I'm looking for them under the table.
He laughs again.
"No, I mean on television. With Charlton Heston. See, God told the Jewish people once. But they wouldn't listen. So he told them twice. But they still wouldn't listen. So he shook the mountain. (He laughs.) *Then* they listened. You see? He gave them the third degree."

He cracks up.

Well, I had a nice talk with the old guy. And I was pretty damn proud of Becky for bringing people like that to the library. That's what I always liked about the Czech movies of the sixties. The young people and the old people were always nice to each other.

You don't see that kind of thing that much anymore.

When we entered the Safeway, Jack kneeled and said his little prayer:

I take refuge in the Buddha.
I take refuge in the Dharma.
I take refuge in the Safeway.

Almost before he finished, the checkers began to tell the people in line: "He's a novelist from New York." Their voices overlapped like shadows on a TV.

111

Joe Henderson appeared quickly, smiling to help put the people at ease.

"Can I help you, Jack?"

"Yes, I was wondering where you keep the bottles of matzo remover."

"Er . . . yes . . . But tell me, Jack, do you remember Carl Braun of the old New York Knicks?"

"Do I remember Carl Braun? Are you kidding me? Does the rabbi pray in the woods?" He turned to me, "Do I remember Carl Braun? I only saw him play every week for four years and I modeled my patented running one-hand push shot after his . . . "

As Jack went on about basketball, Joe gave me a wink which, as a student of business management, I understood immediately. With one quick question, Joe had gotten Jack off his matzo trip and back on the ground.

You don't get to manage a big Safeway if you can't handle people. That's what management's all about. Getting things done through people. The economics of it is secondary.

Chapter 23

JACK'S CLASS WAS SCHEDULED from seven to ten every Tuesday evening for thirteen weeks. The first session fell on June second.

Jack had never taught before, and I thought it was important to make a good impression, so I was disappointed when he decided to take Hark and Grandma Franklin to the first class. I was personally embarrassed, too, because when he walked into the class with Hark beside him and Grandma Franklin on his back, his hands were full so I had to carry his box of matzos.

There were about twenty-five students present. A wide variety. Some hippie types, some neat, long-haired young people, and a good sprinkling of older people from the local community, looking for an outlet for their creative energies.

The first thing Jack does is explain to the class that he's a novelist from New York filling in for the regular teacher who got cancer.

So far, so good.

Then he introduces himself as Dr. Ernest Hemingberg!

Well, the class is uneasy, but when he matter-of-factly writes it on the blackboard and continues, they decide to play along with him, which is all he really wants at the start.

Then he explains how the class will be run—they can write about anything, read it in class, get feedback, no censorship, creative criticism better than negative sniping, anyone who can write a letter can begin to write stories, chief blocks to creativity are emotional fears of facing what might come out, but it's better to face it because it's going to come out anyway, etc. etc.

He's got them so far. They can sense he means well. Except for the Hemingberg bit, he's going over. Then a small crisis. He begins to talk about non-realistic writing. Art doesn't have to follow life and so on. I begin to get uneasy. This path could lead toward Opteema.

An innocent-looking young woman raises her hand. "You say art doesn't have to follow life. But can you tell me, professor, exactly what *is* the difference between art and life?"

"Oh, that's simple," Jack says. "Life is boring."

There's a silence. A few people titter. Jack saves it by adding, "Just kidding. Don't worry about it. We'll get back to that as the course progresses."

She smiles. So far, still so good. His demon is struggling to get out but he's fighting back and improvising around it when he can't contain it.

Then this older man asks him, "What are you working on now, professor, if I may ask?"

"Sure. Only you don't have to call me professor. Just call me Ernie. OK?"

The man smiles. Apparently it's OK.

"Right now I'm working on a movie. You know these movies where an army of giant ants attacks a town?"

They nod yes.

"Well, I'm writing one about an army of giant *uncles* that attacks a town."

They laugh.

"Then I'm going to do a sequel for an Egyptian movie company in which an army of giant *yentas* attacks a town. There's no way to stop them. Finally they call in the air force to bomb them but it doesn't work."

"How do they stop them?" this obese girl asks, smiling.

"They don't."

A few more titters. It's getting dangerous. Jack goes double or nothing. "You know, I don't have to teach here for a living. I used to be chairman of the Humanities Department of a driving school. (A few more laughs. He's getting to them.) The reason I quit was they wouldn't just let me teach writing. I had to double up in a class in 'Reverse.'"

More of them laugh out loud. They're beginning to get the idea. He's a professor who tells jokes. He's *trying* to get them to laugh. They begin to relax a bit.

"I want to emphasize your freedom in here. You can write whatever you like. Don't worry about what constitutes a 'story.' You can re-invent the story. Like the abstract expressionists re-invented painting. They threw out their canvases and framed their palettes."

Just a few anxious laughs. He's getting over their heads.

Then this guy about thirty, with a natty mustache, says coyly, "Do you mean that if we want to, we can paint a mustache on the Mona Lisa?"

"Well, that's been done," Jack says. "I'd like it better if you'd paint the Mona Lisa on your mustache."

They crack up. He's winning. It's obvious. A woman about sixty, nice smile on her face, gray hair knotted neatly in a bun, says, "I've never written before. It seems so hard to make things up. How do you do it?"

"It's not hard. Just don't be afraid to deal with what comes out. Like right now, someone give me a topic and I'll make up a story . . . . Come on, give me the premise . . . "

They're silent for a minute, then this emaciated, long-haired, wild-looking guy ventures, "A flying saucer lands in the desert in Arizona?"

"OK, great." Jack looks up at the ceiling for about ten seconds, then turns back to the class. "A flying saucer lands in Arizona. It's peopled by these little men who are three and a half feet tall. The Earthlings rush out to greet them and learn their wisdom. It turns out they're bores. They all look like little Barry Goldwaters. All they want to talk is business: 'How's the market? Do you have a Merrill-Lynch too?'

"But even though they're boring, they have this superior technology so they take over the Earth. But they're shocked by the way Earthling women dress. Revealing their erogenous zones. Their elbows and their knees. So they force the women to wear basketball knee-pads and elbow-guards. No clothes. Just knee-pads and elbow-guards. Slowly the Earthlings begin to give up screwing and the Earth starts to get depopulated. All the men want to do is get together with the women behind the barn and feel up their knees.

"The story has a happy ending, though. The Jewish hero makes a fortune in knee-pad futures."

Well, he's got them on his side now. And he knows it. So what does he do? He begins to talk about that damned Opteema!

I mean, it was OK at first. They liked him, and they felt that so far it had been an interesting class, but when he went on and on about Opteema they mostly tuned out and waited for him to come back. When he didn't, the natives began to get restless. He noticed, but instead of stopping, he tried harder. This made it worse.

And the classroom circumstances didn't help him either. It seemed that each time he got to an important point, someone would interrupt. Like when he's doing his lead-in about how he tried to change the world by writing his novel and failed because of the loyalty people had to the fantasies they were given as "real" when they were children, this totally stoned-out young guy with thick glasses strays in the door.

"Is this Creative Writing 212?"

"That's right."

"Far out. I'm Vince D'Acosta. I signed up for this class."

There's a quiet moment as the guy walks to an empty chair, notices the whole class is watching him, watches them as he attempts to sit down, misses most of the chair, and falls on the floor.

Everyone laughs as Vince smiles and gets back up. Jack has lost their attention.

"Let's see, where was I?"

Most of them don't remember.

"I think you were talking about your novel," the helpful lady with the gray hair in the bun says. "And I wanted to ask you about that."

"Do you mean, 'Can one change the world through writing?'" Jack says, interested.

"No . . . What I mean is, if you *do* feel you can change the world through writing, is it necessary to get an agent to get started?"

"My uncle wrote a book," the obese girl says, "and he sent it out without an agent."

"Who published it?" a bearded guy with an insolent look on his face says.

"No one."

A retired army type with short hair says, "Tell me, professor, do agents charge for reading manuscripts?"

"Just a second," Jack says, frustrated.

"I'll tell you what I think," stoned Vince says. "I think the biggest problem we got today is drugs. And I know who's behind it."

Before Jack can interrupt, the guy with the beard says, "Who's that?"

"The goddamn Pope, that's who," Vince says. "It just came to me today."

"Well, that's interesting," I say, trying to help Jack who's just watching this now, dumb with disbelief. "It's good to hear a reasonable hypothesis that can be scientifically tested. I'm so tired of dopers spilling out their paranoid raps."

Vince smiles. Some of the other people laugh. This gives Jack a chance to get control of the class. He begins his rap about changing the world by changing the way people imagine it, and he's got some of them listening, but he goes on too long again, and once he gets into pushing the way *he* imagines it, Opteema and Pesseema, this "Isadora Duncan" in her thirties, with heavy make-up, and hoop earrings, and a low-cut black blouse with all these veils and scarves wrapped around her, interrupts him and says, in a sharp tone, "This is all very interesting, but I thought this was a class in writing."

"I've got the first eight pages of a novel on Vietnam," the retired army man says to Jack. "Maybe I could read them and you could tell me whether you think it's publishable."

"I'm talking about *changing the world!*" Jack snaps at the class.

"That's fine for you," the woman with the veils says. "You're already published."

"Publishing doesn't mean shit," the guy with the beard says. "It's just a cop-out way of selling out to the capitalists."

"That's right!" Vince says. "You don't see nothing in the

capitalist press about the Pope and drugs, do you?"

"Do you think drugs help your writing?" the long-haired, thin guy says.

The obese girl says, "My uncle took drugs, and he once sold a story about a talking jeep to this magazine, 'Four-Wheeler.'"

"Just a minute!" Jack shouts. "I was trying to say something."

"You've been talking for two hours!" the veiled woman says.

"Well, he *is* the teacher," the nice, gray-haired woman says.

"Well, this is a writing class," the veiled woman says, "and I paid good money to take it, and we've been here for over two hours and no one's read a thing. I'd like to read my poems."

"Yeah, let her read," the bearded guy says.

"I was trying to finish a story about my uncle," the obese girl says.

"I'm writing a novel about the goddamn Pope," Vince says.

"And I'm trying to *teach* you something," Jack says. And he gets the floor for a minute and begins an analysis of the ways in which what we imagine to be unreal might be real to people from other cultures—dreams, visions, etc.—when Vince pops up and begins to walk out of the class.

Again, Jack loses the thread of his thought. "Where are *you* going?" he says.

"To my car." Vince has a confused look on his face. "I thought the class would only last an hour tonight, man. I left my dog in my car."

"Well, why don't you just bring him back?" Jack says, nodding toward Hark.

"I would, man, but I can't remember where my car is. I better go out and look for it."

He leaves. A young guy in an army fatigue jacket stands and says to Jack, "I'd better split too, man. Enjoyed the class but I gotta get to work. I can only stay for the first hour from now on. I do it for the G.I. bill. It's a good class though." And he leaves.

"I have a short story," a dark-haired, tired-eyed woman,

about thirty, says. "How do I get it copyrighted?"

"I don't copyright anything," the bearded guy says. "I give it away on the streets. To the people. For free. Anyone can *make money* off of writing . . . "

"Look, this business talk is fine for a tavern," the veiled lady says, "but I'm a *poet*. I want to read my work." She pulls out a sheaf of about a hundred ragged-edged pages.

"My mother always put my poems out in the rain," the obese girl says.

I say to the veiled lady, "Why don't you read them first next week?"

"That sounds reasonable," the retired army guy says, trying to help out Jack.

"Let her read now," the bearded guy says.

"I'm trying to *lecture*," Jack says.

"I don't know," the tired-eyed woman says to the bearded guy, "but I find what he says interesting, even if I disagree with it."

"I don't understand very much of it," the gray-haired woman says, "but I find it interesting, too."

"I got some hits off it," the thin, long-haired guy says, "but maybe it's time to close up shop for the night, and go out and get a couple beers. 'Whacko' is playing at the Turntable, and they got this new chick vocalist . . . "

"OK!" Jack says, irritated to the point where I can tell he's about to take the sheath off his tongue. He turns to the veiled lady. "You can read first next week."

"Do you want to put my name down so you'll remember? I took a class with Stanley Ronen at San Francisco State and he always put our names down . . . In fact, I've taken several classes in writing at three different schools, and none of them began like this . . . "

Grandma Franklin is sleeping in her chair in the corner, oblivious to everything. Jack is turning red. He pulls out a piece of paper.

"OK, what *is* your name?"

"Oh, I don't write under my real name."

"Do you *read* under your real name?"

"I don't read *or* write under my real name," she says nastily.

"What name do you write under?" Jack says. *"Sir Philip Sidney?"*

The whole class begins to laugh, but she just stands up and says, with what must seem to her as great dignity, "I write under the name of 'Adoration' and I hope to read first next week when all this street-corner philosophy is finished."

She stomps out the door. The retired army guy tiptoes after her, saying to Jack apologetically, "Gotta run too, Chief. Gotta pick up the missus . . ."

Two other students smile and leave.

"Is anyone here into science fiction?" the obese girl says.

Several people begin a private discussion with her across the classroom, three others pack up and leave, while Jack sits there looking tired, silent as a stone that's crumbling inside.

After the class, Jack stopped to buy a fifth of cheap Scotch and a *TV Guide*. On the way home, I tried to talk to him. "Jack," I said, "this Opteema bit . . . It isn't going over . . ." But he wouldn't listen.

After we dropped grandma off, we found Becky and Wheeler back at our place, sitting in front of the Franklin stove, drinking wine. Jack just walked by them and into his bedroom. Alone with Hark and his fifth of Scotch.

"It didn't work out?" Wheeler said.

I told them what had happened.

"What a bunch of creeps!" Nectarine said.

"It isn't them," Becky said. "It's Jack. He's the brightest guy I know, but every time he gets something going right, he spoils it by talking about that crazy Opteema."

"It's not as crazy as you think," Nectarine said. "Remember, they said Columbus was crazy too."

"They said Galileo was crazy," Wheeler said.

"They said my Uncle Harry was crazy," I said.

"What does that have to do with it?" Becky said.

"He *was* crazy," I said.

"Look at Louis Pasteur," Wheeler said.

"What does *he* have to do with it?" Nectarine said.

"They said *he* was crazy when he injected himself with rabies and bit his son."

We listened to records and drank quite a bit of wine and made a few more desperate jokes to keep from talking about

Jack. But I still couldn't stop *thinking* about him. I was pretty drunk by the time Wheeler and Becky left. Nectarine wanted to comfort Jack, but when she went into the bedroom Jack came out carrying the *TV Guide*. He was wearing his old blue pajamas and was very drunk. He sat down on the rug and thumbed through the program listings. We said nothing to each other until he finished and looked up.

"Anything interesting on this week? We could go over to Wheeler's and watch it together."

"Not really . . . I was looking for an old Carmen Miranda movie . . ." he said, slurring his words slightly.

"You really like them?"

"No."

"Then why do you want to watch one?"

"I don't know."

"You know what I think?" I said, drinking half a glass of wine and beginning to realize how drunk I was too. "I think she's some kind of fertility goddess . . . Like the Earth, with all that fruit coming out of her head . . . I think the Americans turned to her when World War Two made it seem like Judeo-Christian civilization was coming to an end . . ."

"I don't know, Jerr . . ." The skin seemed to hang on his weary face like a sloppy wallpaper job. "I just want to be where everyone in the world likes us again, and they all dance the samba in the streets . . ."

We sat somberly for a couple minutes, and then, surprisingly, his face brightened for a second, as he opened the *TV Guide* and said, "Here, look at this one, Jerr."

He almost toppled over on the rug as he stretched to hand it to me:

> "The Countess of Monte Cristo." (1948) Two Norwegian barmaids (Sonja Henie, Olga San Juan) pose as a countess and a maid at a swank resort. (90 min.)

"Can you picture casting someone with a name like Olga San Juan as a Norwegian barmaid?" he said.

I caught his eyes and, somehow, we began to laugh together and we couldn't stop—a mad, drunken howl of laughter that seemed to swell as it bounced back and forth between us and left us weak on the floor with tears in our eyes.

When we finally quieted, we listened to a Billie Holiday record until I got tired and went downstairs, leaving Jack alone in the living room. As I lay in my bed, I could hear him above me, playing hard rock records, one right after the other, at tremendous volume.

By himself. All through the night. The deafening wail of the rock guitar screaming out like God's ambulance trying to bring relief.

During the silences between the songs I could hear the clomp-clomp of Jack's Quasimoto imitation. But most of the time the music was so loud I couldn't even hear Millicent's father moaning.

Chapter
24

ON THE FIRST SATURDAY IN JUNE, my job at the flea market began. Wheeler and I were going to drive down together. Nectarine was coming too, to fill in for Molla's wife for the day. This Molla character was Wheeler's "business associate" in various ventures. He was a small-time gangster type, originally from Boston. Wheeler told us his name was "Gustave" Molla, but we didn't believe him.

That morning was sunny, mild, and clear, just like every other morning. I was beginning to wonder whether they had clouds in California. When I went upstairs for breakfast, Shoshanna and Jimi were sitting on the floor, painting with watercolors. I looked over Shoshanna's shoulder and I couldn't believe what I saw. Three soft-textured, wide horizontal bars filled the paper. The top one a kind of mauve, the next one rust, and the bottom maroon.

It was a Rothko. An incipient Mark Rothko. And Shoshanna, who was only five years old, had invented it on her own. I got so excited I ran downstairs, grabbed an art book with a Rothko print in it and brought it back up to show her.

"What's that?" she says, looking it over, suspiciously.

"This is a painting by a famous painter named Mark Rothko. And, see, yours is just like his."

She looks at them both, then turns to me with a puzzled, not very pleased, expression on her face.

"What's the matter, Shoshanna? Don't you see they're both the same? See . . . each has three bars across it . . . "

"But they're different!" she insists.

"In what way?"

"Mine's a *house!*"

"Oh . . . er . . . yeah . . . "

I had a lot to learn about dealing with kids.

Anyhow, while Nectarine was preparing to go, smoking her mid-morning half joint, I decided to tell the kids a story to redeem myself. Nectarine had brought home this dull-orange cat that looked like sherbert. Jack had named him Morris. Jimi couldn't say Morris, so he called him Maris.

"This is the story of The Three Little Pigs. Ira, Maris, and Leviathan. Ira and Maris were originally named Izzy and Moe. They lived in New York, but the gentiles didn't like them because they were Jewish and the Jews wouldn't accept them because, no matter how hard they try, pigs can't be kosher. So they moved to California and Izzy and Moe changed their names to Ira and Maris . . . "

"Maris is a cat," Jimi said.

Before I could answer, Wheeler burst in the door ready to go, and when I looked up I noticed that Jack had come out of his bedroom in his pajamas and had been listening to my story. He had dark circles under his mappy eyes. He hadn't been out of the house since his class.

"Not bad," he said. "You have more imagination than you think. You'll be a writer yet."

"You're the writer," Wheeler said. "And it's about time you stopped the crap and got down to work."

"Those that know, don't speak," Jack said.

"Oh, come off it," Wheeler said. "That's OK for some Chinese guy on a buffalo riding off into the sunset, but you're an American from The Bronx."

"Don't knock Buffalo," Jack said. "Grover Cleveland came from Buffalo."

"Let's get out of here before he starts quoting Wittgenstein," Wheeler said, turning to me. "'Whereof we cannot speak, thereof one must be silent,' etc. etc., blah blah, and so forth. It's like a broken record already."

"You know what you don't understand?" Jack said to

Wheeler, suddenly turning very serious. "You don't understand that nothing any person writes will last as long as 'The Three Little Pigs.'"

I tried to change the mood. "You know what *you* don't understand?" I said to Jack. "You don't understand that given enough monkeys with enough typewriters, one of them will eventually write *King Lear*."

"How do *you* know?" he said.

"Because one of them already did it," I said.

Nectarine and Wheeler cracked up and the three of us left Jack to babysit for the kids. As we went out under the blanket that hung over the door, I turned back and I saw the hint of a smile on Jack's face. He might have gotten grumpy whenever Pesseema vibes leaked through the gas mask of his fantasies, but he was still my brother.

In fact, wherever we used to go in The Bronx—to the schoolyard to play basketball, to the YMHA to dance to the jukebox, or to the corner to hang around and tell jokes and tall stories—everyone there knew us, and when they saw us coming they'd always say, "Here come the two brothers."

We're rolling down highway 101 in the van, on the way to the Bay Area. Doing seventy-five, Wheeler at the helm, Nectarine between us. The radio tuned to KSAN, the San Francisco rock station. A song about a man whose mother told him to find people he could trust. And he'd rather trust a country man than a city man. You can tell by the look in his eyes. And Blah, Blah, Blah . . .

Wheeler is rapping away as he drives: "So anyhow, Nect old kid, tell me the truth, did you know that Gabby Hayes was the illegitimate son of President Rutherford B. Hayes?"

"Are you kidding me?"

"Would I kid you? That's how he got into movies. It wasn't his looks."

"Is that really true?"

"No."

She turns to me. "I never know when to believe this guy."

"To tell you the truth, I lie a lot," Wheeler says.

"I'll tell you something that's *really* true," I say to her. "You know Lightning Hopkins, the blues singer?"

"Of course."

125

"Well . . . and this is just between us . . . Lightning Hopkins is the illegitimate son of Gerard Manley Hopkins."

She punches my thigh. I grab her fist.

"Hey, come on . . . It's true."

"Ah, you guys are all nuts," she says, smiling.

"Well, your old man isn't exactly sane," Wheeler says.

"Hey, leave off him. At least he's trying to change the world. That's more than I can say for you, in law school, trying to become a millionaire."

"Don't knock lawyers," Wheeler says. "Franz Kafka was a lawyer." He pulled out and passed a big Safeway truck. "But seriously, I'm getting a little worried about that guy. What the hell does he do in the house all day?"

"He went out to teach," I said.

"I know," Wheeler said. "And he hasn't hardly come out of the house since."

"He's thinking up plans about how to get across to his class," Nectarine said. "And he's thinking up ideas for the new world."

"Oh, come off it," Wheeler said. "Name me one practical idea he's come up with in the month he's been in that house."

"Well," Nectarine said, "he claims right now he's working out a method of crippling the morale of the people in an enemy country during wartime by pinpoint bombing their bowling alleys."

Wheeler and I cracked up.

"You see?" Nectarine said. "You guys encourage him. You talk like he's crazy or something, but you think he's funny so you go along with him and support him."

"You want us not to support him?" I said.

"Well . . . no . . . but if you do go along with him, you should believe in him more . . . I think he thinks you believe in him more than you really do . . . Ah, you guys'll come around once he gets a following."

"Sounds like you're the one who's really supporting him," I said.

"Me?" She seemed startled for a second. "Well . . . sure . . . I mean, what's the alternative? A poodle cemetery?"

I felt there was a hint of uncertainty in her voice that I hadn't heard before. It surprised me, but I let it pass.

"Well, I for one love him like a brother," I said.

Wheeler chuckled.

"But I wish he'd write again," I added.

"You know what he told me the other day?" Wheeler said. "He told me he's going to publish a small man's edition of the Bible in which the feats and accomplishments of those of below-average height will be brought out and emphasized. He says he's going to make a fortune off of short Christians."

We all laughed as Wheeler swung the van onto the approach to the Richmond Bridge.

"You know what he told *me*," I said. "He told me he's fallen in love with a yak."

Even Nectarine had to smile at that. "He told *me* he's going to go to Hollywood and become 'Rabbi to the Stars,'" she said.

Well, we all got to laughing pretty hard, telling "Jack Stories," and Wheeler had tears in his eyes as he drove across the bridge. I felt better than I had in a long time. I think it was seeing the skyline of San Francisco off in the distance over to the right. I know all about skyscrapers. How they mess up the center of the city by pulling all these commuters and traffic into the downtown area, etc., etc. But I still like them in a way. I mean, at least they're *ours*, goddamnit.

And I liked being in traffic again. I liked the security of having all these people around me. In the country there're so few people that you always feel if some madman goes berserk he's going to turn up at *your* house. In the city, at least, you think he'll probably shoot someone else.

"Well, I don't know," Wheeler said. "We can joke about him, but this weird hat trip he's on is pretty crazy if you ask me. I think he's turning into some kind of a 'haterosexual.'"

"It's better than being an ordinary rich lawyer," Nectarine said.

"I'm not going to be an ordinary lawyer," Wheeler said. "I'm going into forensic dentistry."

On the Richmond side, the toll taker was this big black guy with a goatee, listening to loud jazz on a portable radio. I was feeling safer and safer.

Wheeler handed him a buck. Before he gave us the change, he pointed to the radio and said, "Who's that? Who's that?" It was Ray Brown, playing his great bass solo on the "How High

The Moon" cut out of the *Oscar Peterson at the Stratford Shakespeare Festival* LP. I hadn't heard it in years.

"Oscar at the Shakespeare," I said quickly, and the black guy cracked up and said, "Solid," and he reached into the van so I could slap him five, and I did, and I felt like I was home again.

"That guy was all right," Wheeler said, as he pulled away from the tollbooth. "He reminded me of my brother-in-law."

"I thought you didn't like your brother-in-law," I said.

"Reuben?" Wheeler chuckled. "I have nothing against Reuben. He may be nuts, but I like him. He sends me Archie Shepp records. He's trying to convert me." He swung to the left and passed a huge Safeway truck. "Only last week I called him long distance and told him how to make a fortune, but he wouldn't listen to me."

"How's that?"

"I had this idea for selling big words to hipsters in Harlem. A kind of Word-A-Month Club. Like the word for the first month would be 'droll.' Can you imagine the police coming up to these mean black dudes on a street corner in Harlem and telling them to move along, and they begin to answer with sentences like, 'What, are you being *droll*, daddy? *Droll?*'"

"Sounds like there's really a fortune in it," Nectarine said dryly, as I laughed along with Wheeler. Then she said, "You know, in spite of anything you say, you have to admit Jack's been a big influence on your lives."

"I admit it," I said.

"The biggest influence on my life was Clarence 'Frog-man' Henry," Wheeler said.

"Honestly," Nectarine said, "I don't know why I got involved with you guys in the first place. I should've just gotten a job at the mental hospital and fucked the nuts."

Chapter 25

MOLLA'S WIFE COMES up to answer the door to their large, pink, stucco house with rust-shingle roof and two-car garage. She is this fat woman named Norma. She has a towel wrapped over her head and under her jaw. The expression on her face is so sour that I figure either she's in great physical pain or else she has swallowed a tape deck that's playing country and western music and she can't turn it off.

I hoped she had a toothache because one of her cheeks was so much bigger than the other that I figured if she didn't have an abscessed tooth on that side then she must have some kind of weird shrinking-cheek disease on the other.

Molla was behind her, a strong, round, fire-hydrant of a man whom I would describe as tall, dark, and handsome, except for the fact that he was short and ugly.

"Hey, Molla," Wheeler says, "What's the matter with your wife? She got elephantiasis of the face?"

Well, this was pretty crude, even for Wheeler, but Molla thought it was a scream. I didn't know at the time that it was impossible to be cruder than Molla. The only thing that could have even approached him would have been Hermann Goering, in a tutu, toe-dancing.

Wheeler made his apologies to Norma for the joke. I could see that she liked him and hadn't really minded what he said, but I was sorry he'd said it, and from the way he was talking to her I thought he was sorry he'd said it too.

Molla led us through the house while he explained his latest scheme to Wheeler. It involved holding up an antique show in Massachusetts. Molla was from Boston, and he had this weird plan that involved Wheeler dropping nerve gas on the town from a helicopter while Molla and his boys went in and cleaned everybody out. He had some notion that if he could advertise a free barbecue and dance at the same time and place as the antique show, all these black people would show up and when they realized it was a hoax they would riot and in the confusion he could get away.

"Sounds great," Wheeler said, laughing.

Molla continued to expound upon his plan, saying it all depended on "the niggers."

"How can you talk like that?" I said. "Wheeler is married to a black woman."

"And we love her," Nectarine said.

Molla was honestly abashed. "And I *don't* love her?" he said. "I would lay down my life for her."

"Well then, how can you talk about 'niggers' then?" I asked him.

"*She's* not a nigger," Molla said, opening the door to the garage. "She's like a sister to me. Anyone ever calls Becky a nigger, I'd kill him. And Wheeler knows I'm not kidding. Right?"

"He's not," Wheeler said, smiling. "That's the funny part. He's really *not* kidding."

We followed Molla down the three concrete steps into the garage. In the space for a second car, there were these three hand trucks made of iron frames with canvas sides. Like the kind they have in the post office. In fact, when I got closer, I saw "Property of U.S. Postal Service" stamped on their sides. They were filled with hundreds of eight-track tapes. I picked one up. A Bob Dylan album, but with a simple, homemade label.

"What are these?"

They turned to me.

"How come these tapes have funny labels?"

"Because they're funny tapes," Molla said, winking at Wheeler.

"No, I mean it."

"They're rip-off tapes," Wheeler explained.

"I get them from a factory in Nevada," Molla says. "That's how come we can sell them for so cheap."

"But isn't that illegal?"

"Legal? Illegal? Who knows?" Molla said. "They change the laws every day. Look," he put his arm around my shoulder, "who's richer, me or Bob Dylan? You think he gives a shit about me? Or about my wife? Why should I give a shit about him? He's a millionaire!"

"Well, he still should get paid for his work."

"He does. He makes a fortune off every rich kid who goes to Sears and buys a tape for six bucks. I sell them to the poor for two-fifty. This way he gets his music to the people and they still have money left to buy food. Wheeler and I make a few bucks off it, we pay people like you good money for selling the stuff, and who's the wiser?"

"It's like Robin Hood," Wheeler said, smiling.

"Yeah, like Robin Hood," Molla repeated, without Wheeler's irony. "Your friend Wheeler here, he's gonna be a lawyer. Defend the poor. Is Bob Dylan gonna put him through law school? You bet your sweet ass he isn't."

We loaded the tapes into cardboard cartons and piled them into Wheeler's van. Molla came with us when we left. We had to stop at the bottom of his driveway as a pretty, well-endowed girl, about fifteen, wearing tight shorts and a sleeveless sweater, crossed in front of the van.

"*Mar-roan!*" Molla said, shaking his hand in front of him like he'd just touched a hot bowl of manicotti, "When they change the age of consent in this state to sixteen, watch out!"

The flea market was a series of booths, like a small carnival, and one corrugated-metal roofed building, set behind a parking lot.

At the entrance to the parking lot, a girl stood in a booth, taking a quarter admission. We stopped at the booth. Molla got out, walked into the booth, and grabbed a wad of dollar bills from a metal box behind her.

"What's he doing?" I shouted to Wheeler. "Is he nuts?"

"Calm down," Wheeler said. "We own this booth."

"You *what?*"

"Molla and I. We used to rent space here. Then we bought out the guy. We own the land."

Molla got into a hassle with the girl in the booth. He told her she was fired. She began to cry. He re-hired her.

"Gotta keep them on their toes," he said, getting back into the car.

My booth was opposite that of a jive black guy who was also selling cheap tapes. He had on these platform shoes and this tight orange jump suit with straps over his bare shoulders. On his head, he had a big green three-musketeers hat with a green feather. Before Wheeler and Molla went off to the auction in the metal building where Nectarine was going to fill in for Molla's swollen wife, Molla pointed to these huge aluminum cans without labels under the counter of my booth.

"What're those?" I asked.

"Hot crab," Molla said.

"*What?*"

"Hot crab meat," Wheeler said. "We sell it along with the tapes. Seven bucks a can."

"And that's cheap," Molla said. "That's first class crab. Don't ask what we had to go through to get it."

"Just keep it under the counter," Wheeler said. "When someone buys some tapes, you ask him if he can use some crab."

"Only don't just sell it to anyone," Molla said. "You gotta be careful."

"How do I tell?"

"You watch what they buy," Wheeler said. "If they buy Herb Alpert or the Carpenters or something like that, forget it. If they buy something hip, then you spring the crab on them. You have good taste. Just use your judgment. It'll work out."

"Are you sure?"

"What's the matter?" Molla said. "You don't like crab?"

"I love crab."

"Wait til you see next week," Molla said. "We're coming into twenty cases of hot eel meat."

"Oh, great."

"You don't like eel?" Molla said.

"I *love* eel. In fact, there's only one thing I'd rather eat than an eel."

"What's that?"

"Half an eel."

Even Molla had to laugh, and off they went to the auction, leaving me with the hot tapes and the hot crab.

And the black guy across the aisle who was taking away most of my business. The majority of the customers were black and Chicano, and this black guy was blasting out his soul tapes and shouting, "OK, bloods, buy from a brother. Send your money round, but keep it here in town."

Well, after a short while, I see this black guy is killing me. He's selling three tapes to my one (although I'm doing pretty good on the crab). I'm about to tell Wheeler, who comes along with a refill of tapes, one carton on each shoulder, but he walks over to this jive cat and begins to unload the tapes into his booth.

"Wheeler!" I shouted, leaping over the counter and running toward him, "Have you gone nuts? This guy's killing us."

Wheeler began to laugh in that boyish, shoulder-shaking way he has when something really knocks him out. "Didn't I introduce you? This is Jomo. He works for us too."

Jomo shook my hand and smiled. It was that kind of day. The booth next to mine was run by this slim, easy-going man, selling underwear. He must have been about sixty, but he looked younger. Later in the morning, he came over to talk to Wheeler who had just returned from bringing a keg of beer over to the snack bar. (Wheeler and Molla had the beer license, too.)

"This is Henry White," Wheeler said. We shook hands. "Henry was a bomber pilot in World War Two. He doesn't look it, does he? You ever meet a Jewish bomber pilot before?"

"That was long ago," Henry said.

"Henry retired from his army-navy store last year," Wheeler said.

"But I couldn't sit around. So I come here on the weekends, just to keep a hand in it."

"Jerry flew Huey helicopters in Nam with me and his brother."

Henry looked at me like he expected me to say something. When I didn't, Wheeler said to him, "This guy always makes out he's a coward or something."

"Some men are born cowards," I said. "I became a coward

by conviction."

Henry laughed. "You don't like to talk about it now, do you?"

"No . . . I guess not."

"At least Jerry'll admit he was there," Wheeler said. "You should meet his brother, Jack. He won't even admit he was in the army."

"And he was a hero," I said. "They shot off part of his foot when he went into this suicide area to get some wounded guy. He didn't stand a chance."

We talked flying for a while. After Wheeler left, Henry said to me, "Your friend Wheeler, he's gonna be a millionaire."

"You think so?"

"I know so. I've been around. He's got it."

"And Molla?"

"Molla, schmolla. He'll do OK, if he doesn't get arrested. But Wheeler's got the brains."

When Henry went back to his booth, he shouted to me, "Hey, Jerry, you want some socks? I can give you a good deal on these."

He held up a pair of the tube socks without heels.

"No thanks."

"They're guaranteed," he said.

The flea market was a pretty seedy affair on the whole. The people who shopped there were OK, but a lot of them seemed crippled somehow. Not physically crippled, but broken in little ways. Like most of the stuff that was on sale in the shabby booths. I was glad it was me who was there and not my brother.

California was Jack's last chance. He was an American. There was no Nepal he could run to. I knew that. I hoped everything would go OK for him. But I couldn't see how that Opteema idea of his was going to get him anywhere.

I'm an accountant. So I know that you can make a profit. Sometimes even a very good profit. But in life there's no business where you don't have to pay your bills each month.

Nectarine came by during her breaks. Molla's auction was crooked. If he didn't get his price from the poor people on the wooden benches, he would sell the object to one of his shills in the audience. The guy would pick it up, take it outside, go around to the back, and return it.

Nectarine wasn't happy about participating in this. "Molla's a creep," she said to me. "He's just a creep. The only thing we have in common to talk about is that my father's Italian."

"I'm glad that Jack's not here."

"Jack's not anywhere."

"What?"

"Oh . . . I'm just tired . . . But I wish he'd get off his ass."

"He's teaching."

"Big deal."

"What about Opteema?"

"Sometimes I wish he'd pay more attention to his wife and kid and less to Opteema."

"You're just in a bad mood . . . It's the auction."

"Yeah, I know . . . But I keep thinking about Molla. I'd like to see Jack get *him* on Opteema . . ."

She walked over to a booth of crap run by a tall black woman we had befriended. The woman was wearing a long black dress and a colorful kerchief, and these wooden clog shoes held on by rhinestone-studded bands strapped over her feet.

I ran my booth for the rest of the afternoon without any trouble. At closing time, the black woman came over to say goodnight to Nectarine and me. She had on this strange fur coat. It looked like it had been made from the pelts of balding skunks who had Afro hairdos. She spun around, modeling the coat for Nectarine.

"See this coat. This's gorilla fur. I got me a good man with this coat. You get yourself a gorilla fur coat. You'll get yourself a good man."

I expected Nectarine to tell her she already had a good man, but she didn't. Then the lady gave Nectarine her shoes. The ones with the rhinestones on them. Nectarine wore them home.

When we dropped Molla off, we went in to see his wife and we succeeded in cheering her up a bit. As we left, Molla stuck his head in the window of the van and said, nodding at Nectarine, "She don't like me. I can tell."

"You're OK," Nectarine said. "But you're such a wop."

"If you weren't Italian, I wouldn't let you say that."

"If I wasn't Italian, I wouldn't *know* it."

"Look, let's face it, money's the root of all evil. Ain't that so, Wheeler?"

"No," Wheeler said. "In fact, I believe that *lack* of money is the root of all evil."

On the way home, Wheeler treated us to French bread, salami, and good California red wine. We ate and drank (mostly drank) as we drove up route 101. When we came to Hamilton Air Force Base, Wheeler pulled off the freeway, parked, and ran over to base headquarters. We ran after him. We were all pretty drunk.

"I want to report a U.F.B.," Wheeler shouted at the astounded desk sergeant.

"Don't you mean a U.F.O.?" the sergeant said.

"Of course not," Wheeler said. "Anyone can spot a U.F.O. I just saw an Unidentified Flying Butcher."

Chapter
26

IT WAS NOON WHEN I AWOKE. The blackboard read:

CAME NOT BY USURA
MATZO BALLS

Jack was seated on the floor, telling the kids a story about a Jewish King Midas. Everything he touched turned to matzo.

Jack had some vomit caked on his shirt. He turned to me. "Is there a fine for slapping the president?"

I forced a smile. I didn't like it when he started these "President" jokes. It was usually a sign he was in a bad place.

Nectarine walked in, carrying a bundle of groceries from the Safeway.

"Well, I see the lady of the house is back," Jack said. "I wonder if she's talking to me?"

"I wonder if you're going to get off your ass today."

Nectarine's tone reminded me of yogurt when it turns green.

"I can't help it if I sit a lot," Jack said. "In my last incarnation I was a chair."

"Very funny!" Nectarine said, unloading the groceries.

"What's this?" I said. "Clouds over Opteema?"

"You know what he did last night?" Nectarine said to me. "You know what your wonderful brother did? He pissed on my cat."

"Big deal," Jack said. "It didn't hurt him."

"I didn't say it hurt him. I just don't like the *idea* of it. That's all." She turned to me. "Why doesn't he get out of the house during the day?" Then back to Jack. "Why don't you come out and work in the garden with me?"

"I can't. When I was a boy I was bitten by a Swiss chard."

She mixed a can of frozen orange juice with water in our yellow plastic container.

"You Pesseemans are too concerned with *doing*," Jack said, slowly standing up and stretching. His eyes were bloodshot. His face looked lightly treaded, like an old radial tire that had gripped the road for too many years. "Pascal said half the world's problems are caused by people not being able to sit still. I'm practicing *not doing*."

"You don't have to practice," Nectarine said. "You're already an expert at it."

"Oh, yeah? You think I'm not productive because I won't work in the fields like Tolstoi or something. Well, it just so happens that I'm working out a new form of meditation. I'm trying to listen to the William Tell Overture without thinking of the Lone Ranger."

"That's just great," Nectarine said.

"You think it's easy? Try it some time."

"Why don't you try writing some time?"

"I am writing. My autobiography. It's called *Popes I Have Known*."

Nectarine placed the yellow container of juice in the refrigerator. Jimi came up to me, followed by Shoshanna. His stuffed giraffe had a handkerchief tied around its neck.

"It has a sore throat," Shoshanna explained.

I took it and examined it in my best medical manner. "This doesn't look too bad. I think if we rub some mayonnaise on it, it should clear up by tomorrow."

"You should get a job," Nectarine said to Jack.

"I *have* a job. I'm a professor."

"I mean a *real* job. One that'll get you out of the house during the daytime."

"You should talk. When was the last time *you* had a real job."

"Look, man, when I was in high school, I had the worst

job in the world. Boxing groceries in the Chicago Safeway."

"Oh, yeah, when I was in high school I had an even worse job. Boxing kangaroos in The Bronx Zoo."

"You see?" Nectarine said to me. "You can't talk to him."

"She doesn't see my real work," Jack said. "I'm developing an IQ test for kids based on kindness."

Just then we heard this mooing and scuffling outside. I ran to the window. "Holy Jesus!" I turned to Nectarine who was putting the canned goods into the cupboard. "You left the gate open. They're right here on the lawn. Between the house and the fence."

"What are *they*?" Jack said.

"I don't know. They look like male cows."

"Jesus Christ!" Jack said. "What next? Mail cows. No wonder it takes a week for a letter to get to New York."

"Not *mail* cows. *Male* cows! Like *big boy* cows."

"*Big boy cows*?" Nectarine said. "Really, you guys are too much!" She walked up to the window. "What's the matter with you? Don't you ever go to the movies? Those are steers. Why don't you just go outside and shoo them out the gate?"

"Are you nuts?" Jack said. "He might start a stampede. They could knock the house over."

"Don't talk to me about cowboy movies," I said to Nectarine. "Do you know I once saw Gene Autry, live, at the rodeo at Madison Square Garden?"

"They had rodeos at Madison Square Garden?"

"You're damn right they did. We weren't as cut off from nature in New York as you other people think."

"Well, Gene Autry, why don't you go out now and get them off my lawn?"

"Why me?"

"You found them."

"Are you nuts? They may be vicious."

"They won't hurt you."

"That's easy enough for *you* to say. You don't have to deal with them. You're a mother."

"Oh, come on . . ."

"Let Jack do it. Maybe on Opteema, male cows are nice."

Jack looked out the window. "Uh, uh. Those look like oxen to me. I'm not gonna mess with an ox . . ."

"They're *steers!*" Nectarine said.

"What *is* an ox?" I said. "A kind of cow?"

"I think it's some kind of buffalo or something," Jack said.

"They're trampling my front lawn!" Nectarine said.

"Where's the encyclopedia?" Jack said.

"Let's just get them the hell out of there," Nectarine said.

"We *will*," Jack said. "But first we have to find out what we're dealing with here."

"I don't think you unpacked them yet," I said. "They're probably somewhere in that pile of cartons of books in your bedroom."

Jack went into the bedroom and began to open cartons.

"This is too much," Nectarine said. "I can't take this anymore. I noticed this morning that my pussy is getting gray . . . I'm thinking about getting a wig."

She strode out of the house and, while Jack looked for the encyclopedia, the kids and I watched her shoo the steers out the gate.

Chapter 27

FOR THE NEXT FEW WEEKS we drifted along the surface of the pea soup of life on our little square acre of toast. Jack's classes were very successful except for the last hour when he would get into his "commercial."

I remember one class in particular. We arrived with our regular party of three: Jack and Hark and me. We'd decided it was kinder to let grandma sleep at home. I was carrying the matzos because Jack had brought this hamper. It was made of coils of woven straw. I guess you could call it a snake-basket hamper since it was shaped like the kind of basket snakes come out of when the guy plays the flute. Only this one was much larger. Almost as tall as Jack.

He set it on the right side of his desk. Hark lay down on the left. Jack began the class with a series of "super" jokes about a fictitious Polish grandfather of ours named "Pilchek" who was supposedly the janitor of a building in The Bronx. Then he gave a short lecture on the heritage of language: "The English language is not just a bunch of words like a bunch of tomatoes in the Safeway. The English language has developed organically over hundreds of years and, through a process of trial and error—a kind of Darwinian survival of the fittest—it has come to embody all the wisdom that the English-speaking peoples have accumulated over centuries . . . That is to say, let's face it, it doesn't contain much wisdom . . . "

Well, this upset several English majors (which was Jack's aim, by the way. That's the way he would teach. By telling jokes and half-truths he would force the class to come to terms with, and to articulate, what *they* believed.)

The natty guy with the mustache was particularly disturbed. "I won't have this," he said. "You can't cast aspersions on the English language. I'll have you know my great-uncle was in the British House of Lords."

"Well, I'll have *you* know my Grandfather Pilchek was in the Polish House of Supers," Jack said triumphantly.

Then this pretty young woman, with long, wheat-colored hair, asked him, "Do you know how to cure a writer's block?"

"Sure. Just say five 'Hail Marys.' Then if that doesn't work, try ten 'Help Me Rhondas.'"

Even the natty guy had to laugh. Then we listened to the students read their stories and Jack, as always, captivated them by his comments. He could, after one hearing, put his finger on whatever was giving a student difficulty, and tell him this in a way the student could accept. At times he would point out the very sentence where second draft stopped and first draft returned. The students loved it. It was like watching a jazz musician improvise around a tune he'd never heard before.

On this particular night, the student on the G.I. bill who could only stay for half the class read a story about Vietnam. It was one of the best we heard, a stunning mixture of random violence and drugs that seemed to explode out of some deep place inside of him with a brutal and almost overwhelming nightmarish power.

As with the other Vietnam stories, Jack let the class discuss it, but he didn't say a word. In the past, they had pushed him into responding and each time he went into an Opteema trip and the class was over. After a few times they had begun to understand this pattern and they had stopped trying to get him to respond when a Vietnam war story was read.

On the first night of the snake basket, Jack began a new routine which he was to continue throughout the class schedule. He waited until late in the class to talk about Opteema, and then, when he saw that he had lost their attention, he took off the cover of the hamper, climbed inside, and didn't come out until they all had gone home.

This became the pattern of his class closings. But the students kept coming back each Tuesday. In his despair over getting his Opteema message across, he was blind to how much he was giving the students by joking with them, by listening to them, and by helping them to express themselves on Earth through their speaking and their writing.

He began to drink more. And to spend more time inside the house. Alone with Hark.

And he began to hint at more desperate ways of getting his message across.

About ten days later, I stayed over in San Francisco on Sunday night with this woman I met at the flea market. She was pretty crazy, but I don't see how she fits in here so I won't go into it.

Well, I didn't get back home till the following Thursday about noon. Becky was there with Shoshanna, watching Jimi who was lying in his little bed in his little room. He had an earache. He thrashed about in his first taste of bitter pain, kicking his legs out in indignation. His face was frantic with disbelief. It was terrible to see.

"The doctor gave him an antibiotic," Becky said. "But it takes time to work."

Becky motioned for me to follow her into the kitchen.

"This is awful," I said.

"You don't know the half of it. It's your brother and Nectarine."

"Are they OK?"

"Well . . . I don't know . . . It's been a strange day."

"What *happened?*"

"I didn't get all the details. All I know is that Nectarine fucked the water commissioner and your brother got arrested."

Chapter 28

WE STAYED WITH LITTLE JIMI until, through the mercy of medicine, he finally fell asleep. It was nice to see the pain smoothed out of his face which had looked older when he was awake—lined and somehow, sadly enough, wiser.

We left Shoshanna where she had fallen asleep on a blanket on the floor next to Jimi's little bed and we walked quietly into the kitchen.

"That was hard to take," I said.

"That's life," Becky said. "Short periods of time between visits to the dentist."

Becky set a small fire under the coffee. "Wait till he asks you how old he'll be when you die," she said.

"What do you say?"

"Sixty-eight," she laughed.

I noticed the message on the blackboard for the first time:

IT IS AN ILL WOMAN
THAT BLOWS NOBODY ANY GOOD

It was a bad sign.

Then Nectarine crashed in, circles under her eyes, her hair tangled and flying about like she'd just returned from The Medusa Sisters' Beauty Parlor.

"What a day! In all of history, this is it. The worst. How's Jimi? He OK?"

"Yeah," Becky said, and told her what had happened. "On top of it all, Rusty got a flat on the freeway."

"How's Jack?" I said.

"Oh, the Prince! . . . He's OK. As usual. Just a couple cuts and a black eye. Wheeler got Dr. Freudenberg to go to the police station and say that Jack was his patient and that he was a little unbalanced but that he wasn't dangerous. So they let him go in Freudenberg's custody. Lefty didn't press charges."

"Lefty?"

"He's the water commissioner," Becky said.

"Jesus Christ!" I said to Nectarine. "How could you fuck the goddamn *water commissioner?*"

"Well, I had to fuck *somebody.*"

"Don't you see the symbolism? Water is the opposite of the goddamn wasteland."

"Oh, come off it . . . "

"No, I mean it. Just because Jack acts like a clown here with us, you forget he's an author. Authors think that way. They might be nuts, but that's the way they see things."

"Well, what about *me?* Does he ever see me?"

"He wants to save the world."

"Then he should have married it."

"Ah . . . Anyhow, why'd he get arrested in the first place?"

"He's out of his mind." She turned to Becky. "And Wheeler encourages him."

"I know," Becky said.

"You know what your darling brother did? He found out I was fucking the water commissioner . . . "

"How'd he find out?"

"Well, we got these crabs. I tried to tell him it was from some pants I bought at the Salvation Army, but he knows they clean the stuff first . . . Anyhow, it came out. So what does he do? He and his friend Wheeler? They go to the Safeway and they get all these cardboard cartons. And then they stay up all night painting them silver. And then they make this kind of knight's suit out of them, and Jack puts on the damn thing (she begins to chuckle) and he gets Wheeler to paint all these big words on it—words like 'excoriate' and 'exculpate' and 'exonerate' and 'amulet,' and who knows what else. And then Wheeler drives him to town and he marches in there in this crazy suit, and he attacks the water commissioner."

I tried to keep a serious expression, but I couldn't. Becky started to laugh too. And then Nectarine. Soon, all three of us were laughing like madmen.

When Nectarine finally caught her breath, she said, trying to keep a straight face, "The suit was so clumsy, he could hardly move. Then, when they heard the scuffle, the fire commissioner and the building commissioner and a couple other kinds of commissioners all ran in and they held him down while Lefty beat the shit out of him."

She cracked up again. We couldn't help but join her.

"I mean, what can you do with a guy like that?" Nectarine said, her face softer now.

She sipped at the hot coffee. Then she began to weep softly. I felt like crying too, but I swallowed my tears. We sat quietly together at the table for a few minutes, thinking our own thoughts. Then Nectarine went inside to take a look at Jimi. Right after she came back, Jack limped in. He had a big mouse under his black right eye, a small bandage over his right eyebrow, another on the left side of his jaw, and some dried blood on his mouth.

He came into the kitchen without saying a word and sat on the floor with his back against the wall. After a few awkward silent moments, he said softly, almost to himself, "Do you think everybody's a secret tap dancer?"

When no one responded, he continued, quietly, "I mean, you know, sometimes when I'm in an elevator by myself, or an empty room, I can't help it, I just start doing all these wild steps . . . I don't know where they come from . . . I just invent them on the spot . . . "

Silence.

Then Jack said, "How could she do it? I mean I know I get self-absorbed for a few days at a time, but our sex was good."

And Nectarine said to Becky and me, "That's not the point. You know what this guy did after the last time we made love? He got on the floor on his hands and knees and made like he was wagging his tail . . . I mean, how can you deal with a guy that wags his tail after you ball him?"

Silence.

"If only it wasn't the water commissioner," Jack said. "I mean, couldn't she have fucked the sewer commissioner or something?"

"You see?" I said to Nectarine. "I *told* you. He thinks that way."

"It's not like I have it so easy with women," Jack said. "Do you know when we were in New York I once got so desperate to meet somebody I took an ad in the personals column of the *New York Review of Books*. I only got one reply. It was from a woman I used to date."

Even Nectarine had to smile. I mean, he looked so damn *funny*, sitting there on the floor, with his bandages and his cuts, telling these stories of his.

"And just this week I was on the verge of my greatest invention. I had this idea for a dryer you could use for your clothes and for salads. It had three settings: Cottons, Synthetics, and Lettuce."

We laughed again. He was working. I'd seen him like this so many times. Change the space we were in by using only words.

"And I had this idea for a porno book for kids: *Tush in Boots*."

We smiled.

"And if that went over, I was going to do a sequel: *Nectarine and her Wonder Tushie*."

Nectarine got up and sat next to him on the floor. She stroked his bandages gently with the tips of her fingers.

"I'm sorry, Jack . . . I guess those guys really worked you over . . ."

"It wasn't too bad . . . But they seemed like a bunch of Nazis the way they jumped on me when I was down."

"Now just one cotton-pickin' minute," I said. "The Nazis might talk tough, but you have to admit they never hurt anybody!"

Everyone laughed.

"How can you joke about something like that?" Becky said, still chuckling.

"As long as someone keeps joking about it, no one's going to forget," I said.

Nectarine leaned over and kissed Jack on the mouth. They

stood up and walked off to the bedroom together, arms around each other's shoulders, and somehow, to me, they looked like two kids who'd gotten caught out in the rain.

When they were gone, Becky and I relaxed.

"You want a tuna fish sandwich?" she asked. "I'm going to make one for myself."

"Sure. I'll make the toast. I'm starving. Why are Jews so into food anyhow?"

"I don't know . . . Maybe it's because they live near delicatessens." Becky mixed the tuna fish with mayonnaise in a large yellow bowl. "You know, you should really get your brother to come to the temple."

"He won't do it. Abraham Lincoln was shot in the temple."

"Seriously . . . "

"Are you kidding? Didn't you hear? It's dangerous to be Jewish now. The president just banned matzos after a report that Jews were snorting the crumbs through dollar bills to get high."

"You better watch out," she laughed. "You're sounding more like your brother every day."

Chapter 29

"ANYONE WANT TO COME to the Salvation Army?" Nectarine asks Wheeler, Becky, Jack and me. We're sitting in our living room sipping cold California chablis. Listening to Bobby Bland. Jimi and Shoshanna are on the floor, finger-painting. It's a warm summer afternoon. Almost no humidity. They don't have humidity in Sonoma County. They send it all back to The Bronx where the people blame it on the mayor.

We'd been playing a game: who could name the most people named Meyer.

"Meyer Levin, the novelist," Jack had said.
"Meyer Davis, the bandleader," Becky said.
"Meyer Baba, the religious leader," I said.
"*Meyer* Baba?" Nectarine said.
"That counts," Jack said.
"Then how about Meyer Kovski, the Russian poet?" Wheeler said.
"That counts," I said.
"Then what about Meyer Daley of Chicago?" Jack said.
"That counts," I said.
"Meyer Alioto of San Francisco," Wheeler said.
"Meyer Lindsay of New York," Becky said.
"Wait a minute. That doesn't count," Wheeler said.
"How come?" Becky said.
"He's no longer the Meyer."

Anyhow, I decided to go to the Salvation Army with Nectarine and the kids. Wheeler and Becky were going to the city to the ballet.

"Do you like the ballet?" Wheeler asked Nectarine.

"Sure . . . But I like barefoot dancing better," she said. "Do you like barefoot dancing, Wheeler?"

"I prefer barefoot singing," he said.

Nectarine asked Jack, "Want to come with us?"

"No. I think I'll stay home. I'm making some big plans."

She turned to the rest of us to plead her case.

"You know, he's been out here for months and he doesn't even know the names of the birds or trees."

"Jack said, "In Eastern European Yiddish there's only two names for flowers, rose and violet. And there's no names for wild birds."

"What's that supposed to mean?"

"That my ancestors weren't into nature. They lived in cities and towns."

"Soon, everyone'll be living in cities," Wheeler said.

"Then everyone'll be Jewish," Jack said.

"That'll be just great," Nectarine said. "Then who'll grow the food?"

"No one grows the food anymore," Jack said. "It comes from the Safeway."

"Really!" Nectarine said. "You ought to do things with us. You should be more of a parent to Jimi."

"I'm giving Jimi the one thing I always wanted as a kid and never had."

"What's that?" Wheeler said.

"A lazy father."

"Ah, you can't talk to him," Nectarine said. "He turns everything into a joke and he thinks he's being some kind of a mystic."

"You either have to be a mystic or a pessimystic," Jack said.

"I think he's some kind of Buddhist," Wheeler said, egging Jack on.

"I am," Jack said. "In fact, my ambition is to be the first neurotic Buddha."

"Well, you're halfway there," Nectarine said. "You're

already neurotic."

She took Shoshanna and Jimi by the hands and walked out the door. I followed. Millicent met us at the gate.

"I don't mean to intrude," she said to me, "but do you sleep in the basement?"

"Yes, I do."

"Have you ever checked how high the ceiling is?"

"Six feet."

"Oh . . . Oh, dear . . . I don't think that's high enough. You better not let any strange people into your house."

"Everyone who comes into our house is strange," Nectarine said.

"My brother says there are no more normal people."

"Oh . . . Well, all I meant was one of them could be a building inspector. Your house could be condemned if your basement ceiling is only six feet high."

"That rule doesn't apply to us," Nectarine said. "We're on the metric system."

We walked away. The kids were picking ripe blackberries from a high hedge alongside the road just past Millicent's house. We stopped to join them. The juice of the berries was warm and sweet. Across the road, down behind our house, I could see the Carmen Miranda Memorial Flagpole. Jack had been neglecting the ceremony. The fruit was dry and rotten. Flies buzzed around it.

Millicent's father began to moan. I worried about Jack. Except for his classes, he continued to stay inside the house practically all the time. The only person he spent time with outside was Hark. His class was doing well, but the Opteema lectures weren't going over at all.

One night, after he'd gotten really drunk, I had heard him shuffling around under the ornamental plum tree, up by the fence on the road. I walked over to him. There was a full moon. Millicent's father was moaning. It almost seemed like the old man was howling at the moon.

In the silver light, I could see tears in Jack's eyes.

"What's the matter?"

"Millicent's father . . . That goddamned moaning."

He took a long swig from the almost empty fifth of Scotch. Then he threw the bottle toward Millicent's house. It hit in an apple tree and fell harmlessly to the grass with a tiny thud. He began to bawl. He kneeled down, with his head in his hands. I kneeled next to him. I put my arm on his shoulders.

"I can't stand it anymore, Jerry. Someone should teach old people . . . It isn't fair that they wind up like this . . ."

"What can anyone say?"

He answered softly, as he continued to sob, not looking at me, "It's OK to live on Pesseema if that's what you want to do . . . But when you die, you gotta switch to Opteema . . . You gotta, Jerry . . . Death is too terrible on Pesseema . . . You need to believe in magic when you're gonna die . . . I can't stand it anymore. I just can't . . ."

Nectarine's voice pulled me back to Earth. "I don't understand him . . . What does he do in there all day? He isn't writing. He isn't marking papers. He isn't doing *anything*."

"Yes he is," I said. "He's suffering."

She didn't answer. She looked especially lovely that day, her blond hair held in by a navy blue scarf studded with small golden stars, the purple juice of the sweet berries staining her teeth and spilling out over her lips, the oak tree leaves in the distance behind her trembling in a little wind-dance choreographed by John Coltrane.

As we stood in the middle of the road waiting for the kids, I looked back toward our house and through the living room window I could see Jack tap-dancing while Becky and Wheeler watched.

Nectarine loved the Salvation Army store. I think she would have moved in if they'd let her. I went to look at the shelves of books in the corner.

I thought of Jack tap-dancing in the house. At least it was better than the damned Quasimoto imitations that he was doing more and more. They'd begun to give me the willies.

"Hey Jerr, look at these."

It's Nectarine at the used pajama table. Holding up these old pale-orange men's pajamas for me to see. The shirt has dark red flowers printed on it.

"You want me to buy these for you?" she asked.

"Are you kidding? Someone else's pajamas?"

"What's wrong with that?"

"They probably belonged to a wino with leprosy."

"They sterilize them."
"Yeah. They use the grill at the Taco Bell."
"Oh, come on . . ."
"You know what I'm going to do if I get rich? I'm going to take you over here and give you ten dollars and say, 'Go wild!'"
She laughed. "Look at what else I found."
She held out a used electric toothbrush with frayed bristles.
"Are you crazy?"
"It's not for *us*. It's for the cat."
"Oh . . ."
When we left the store, Shoshanna was holding the toothbrush. Jimi was carrying a little brown truck with no wheels. Nectarine was wearing a shocking-green bathrobe.
"Can I ask why you're wearing a bathrobe on the street in California in August?"
"It's no longer a bathrobe. I bought it for the rainy season. It's now my new winter coat. I like it better than my old raincoat. My old raincoat made me lean forward."
"But it's not waterproof."
"Well, it doesn't rain that much anyway."
When we got home, Jack was sweating as he practiced his tap dancing, clicking his heels together out to one side, and then, quickly, out to the other. As usual, Hark was there watching stoically. When he saw us, Jack stopped dancing and bounced into the kitchen. Nectarine and the kids walked right by him, toward the cat. They sat down in the corner with him and began to try to get him to hold still while they brushed his teeth. Nectarine didn't comment on Jack's dancing. He didn't comment on her bathrobe.

The sign on the blackboard said:

THE TINTERN ABBEY-ULATION
OF THE BELLS, BELLS, BELLS.

I changed it to:

THE TEN-TEN TABULATION
OF THE BILLS, BILLS, BILLS.

Jack laughed and changed it to:

MITZI DANCING SWEEPS NATION.

EPIDEMIC SPREADS!
5000 MITZI DANCERS ARRESTED
OUTSIDE WHITE HOUSE.
"Mitzi dancing?"
"I can't explain it yet . . . I'm just working it out. But this is it. I know it, Jerr. This is *it.*"
He headed for the door with Hark.
"Where're you going?"
"Oh, man, I feel so great, I'm gonna hook up grandma's horse and then get some fresh fruit for the Carmen Miranda hat from Joe Henderson at the Safeway . . . This is *it!*" he shouted as he walked out.
"Opteema here we come!"

Chapter
30

JACK IS TALKING TO A STUDENT who has not come to class since the first week but has just showed up at our house. Jack won't let him on the property. He keeps the guy on the road and talks to him through the gate.

"I wanted to get in touch with you, man," the guy says, "but you're a hard dude to get a hold of."

"You could have contacted me before the class was almost over."

"Yeah, well, I don't want to put all the blame on you . . ."

"That's OK. That's what a mother is for."

"Well, look, man, I have this writer's block. Do you know anything I can do for it?"

"Yeah. Say five 'Hail Mitzis.'"

The guy says, "That's fucked, man," and sulks off to his car.

But Jack didn't mind. He was chipper and bouncy, filled with energy. Had hardly slept all week as he planned his Mitzi dancing. He was up when I went to sleep and awake when I awoke. He hitched Jefferson to grandma's trailer every morning and performed the Carmen Miranda Memorial Flagpole ceremony twice each day, complete with fresh fruit from the Safeway and an energetic samba with Hark. I had seen him like this before. Filled with nervous energy. Optimistic for eighteen hours a day. It was when his novel came out.

Now he had invented Mitzi dancing. That's why the blackboard had said, EVERYONE IS A SECRET TAP DANCER, for the past two weeks.

That's why, for the coming Saturday night, he had rented a hall (Well, he and Wheeler, actually. It was Wheeler's money.) for the first session of what he expected to become an overnight sensation—Mitzi dancing!

But what was this Mitzi dancing? I had found out the weekend before. When we went over to Wheeler's house to watch an exhibition NFL football game on TV.

Jack was carrying his "football packet" in one hand and a box of matzos in the other when we walked into Wheeler's large living room. Wheeler was sitting at a table, going through some accounts for his business that I had worked up and evaluated for him. Doctor Freudenberg was at the bookcase looking at the titles. Becky was sewing something at the machine in the corner.

"So you're weakening," she said to Jack. "You're going to watch TV."

"The body can handle small amounts of pollution," he said.

I turn on the TV. There's this Dorothy Lamour type, in an old technicolor movie. She's wearing a sarong, standing in front of a fake palm tree, talking to a Latin-lover type. "Don't be alarmed," she says, warmly and gently, putting her arm around his shoulder. "It may not be the plague."

I switched to the game.

The Doc came over to watch. He was in his forties, hair thinning at the top, a neat goatee on his chin, his body thickening at the waist.

"Have you started writing again, Jack?" he said.

"Nope. I've got something better cooking. I'll tell you at the half."

Wheeler closed his books and joined us. Jack opened his football packet and passed out the penalty flags and whistles. Oh, I guess I didn't explain that. You see, when we'd watch a game, Jack would make sure each of us had a penalty flag and a whistle. Then we'd try to spot a penalty on each play. When you saw one, you'd throw your flag and blow your whistle. If it turned out you were right, and you were the first one to blow your whistle, everyone would give you a quarter. If you were wrong, you had to give everyone else a quarter.

Even the Doc took a whistle and a flag, although he seemed a little embarrassed by them. He held them out away from himself, the way he'd hold a baby without a diaper that someone gave him to keep for a minute at the Safeway.

The game had started.

"I think you should stick to your writing," the Doc said. "Writing is your real work."

"Offsides!" Jack shouted, throwing his flag on the floor and blowing his whistle.

But the officials didn't call it. Jack gave us each a quarter.

"You guys are nuts," Becky said, laughing.

"No, really," the Doc said to Jack, "I think you should begin another novel."

"I am beginning one. It's called *The Brothers Shrinkamazov.*" I mean seriously . . ."

"I *am* serious. It's about these three brothers, Id, Ego, and Superego Shrinkamazov. Id, he's the youngest. And he's always galavanting about, fucking up, out of control, ruining the family name, wanting everything he sees. And then there's the oldest, Superego Shrinkamazov. He's like a father to the others, always getting on Id's ass, 'Do this! Don't do this!' Until, just when they're about ready to go at each other and have it out, Ego Shrinkamazov, the middle brother, steps in and he says, 'Now boys, let's be reasonable.'"

"Pass interference!" Wheeler shouted, blew his whistle, threw his flag (it hit the Doc—Wheeler apologized).

Wheeler was right. We each gave him a quarter.

"What's this Mitzi dancing?" Becky said.

"It's the form the Buddha has to take so he can be accepted by Americans," Jack said.

"The Buddha's already appeared in a form Americans can accept," Wheeler said. "Money."

"If you like the Buddha so much, why don't you go to Nepal?" Becky said.

"Are you kidding?" Jack said. "There are no third basemen in Nepal. Besides, it wasn't Nepal that stood up and saved your people from Hitler, and don't you forget that."

"Very interesting," the Doc said, stroking his goatee, but

he didn't elaborate.

"My people?" Becky said. "Aren't they your people too?" Jack didn't answer.

"Tell the truth," Becky said, "is there any better people on the Earth than the Jews?"

"Yes, there is," Wheeler said. "The Druids."

"Oh, come on . . ."

"No, I mean it. It's better to be a Druid. You can freak out your whole neighborhood. You put big rocks on your lawn in weird formations. Try to use them to predict eclipses . . ."

We had a good time together, watching the game. Even the Doc enjoyed it. He made a pretense of subtly helping Jack to give him a professional cover for being there with us, but we knew he wanted to be one of the boys. And we were glad to have him. Even if he never did throw his flag and call any penalties.

At the half, Jack explained his plan. "Mitzi dancing is when any large group of people tap-dance together in a single place at the same time to a local radio station playing top 40 tunes. Wheeler and I rented a hall for next Saturday. We also bought 400 earphone radios. You know what they are?" he asked me.

"I don't think . . . wait, do you mean those kind where each earphone has a little antenna that sticks up off it?"

"That's it," Wheeler said. "Looks like rabbit ears."

"Or insects," the Doc said.

"Or Martians," Becky said.

Jack said, "Anyhow, the way it works is everyone wears these earphones with the antennas sticking up. And they're all tuned to the same station. And everyone's wearing hard-soled shoes."

"Eventually they'll all wear tap shoes," Wheeler said.

"Yeah," Jack continued, "but for the present, hard-soled shoes'll have to do. Well, OK, they're all tuned to the same station, and just as each song starts, they all yell, 'Hail Mitzi!' in unison and begin to tap-dance like mad. And then when the song ends they all stop in unison."

"The beauty of it is they can't hear the tapping or the 'Mitzi!' because of the earphones," Wheeler said. "Only the music."

"But the people watching, all they can hear is the tapping,"

Jack said. "No music. Just a shout of 'Hail Mitzi!' and all these people with earphones and antennas tap-dancing like mad in the silence. And somehow they all start and stop in unison. It'll be like magic. And they can do it anywhere. On the steps of the capitol building. Anywhere . . ."

"It sounds nuts to me," Becky said.

Well, I was sorry she had said that. Both the Doc and I had our doubts, but we could see there was no point in trying to talk to Jack when he was so excited.

He was kind of desperate, if you know what I mean.

But Becky goes right on, to Wheeler, "How can you encourage him in this?"

And when Wheeler just smiles and shrugs, she says, "It must have cost thousands of dollars."

"You stay out of this," Jack says sharply.

"No, I won't."

"We're gonna get thousands of people being crazy and having a good time together," Jack said. "We're gonna blow out this whole Pesseema hypnosis that's got everyone so afraid of dying and of old people. We're gonna bring back magic. And it's gonna spread to the whole world. And it'll be our country that started it."

"I still say it's nuts."

"In two years we're gonna have Ingmar Bergman tap-dancing," Jack said.

"If it's magic you want, you ought to stop this craziness and go to Togoland where my brother was in the Peace Corps," Becky said. "They have a twin society there. Every year they march through the town—a parade of the twins. You'd be honored. Twins are magic there."

"God damn it! Do you think I'm doing this for *honor!*" He stood up and stomped out of the room. Then he stuck his head back in the door and shouted, "And don't talk to me about Togoland! Charlie Parker and John Coltrane weren't any fucking 'Togos.' They were Americans. And I'll tell you something else. When push comes to shove, I'll stick up for American black people against fucking Togos any day of the week."

He stomped out of the house, slamming the door behind him. He left so fast, he didn't even take his box of matzos.

They were sitting there on the floor at the edge of his chair.

"You don't have any faith in anything," Wheeler said to Becky. He got up from his chair and headed for the door. "If Karl Marx had gotten off his ass and gone Mitzi dancing the whole world would be a better place. We're going to get everybody into Carmen Miranda space. Whole towns'll be dancing together again in the streets."

"The secret of Carmen Miranda is she made the best of what she was given!" I shouted after him as he walked out of the room.

Well, I was pretty surprised to hear a person like Wheeler talking like that. I knew his feelings were hurt because he had invested a lot of money in something we didn't believe in, but I hadn't thought that Jack could suck him onto an idealistic trip, even for a little while. I guess it was Wheeler's attraction to things that were crazy and out of control that was at the bottom of it, really.

Well, we turned off the TV and put away the flags and whistles. The Doc and I couldn't get very interested in the second half of the game.

"Jack didn't mean to shout at you," I said to Becky. "He'll be back later to apologize."

"I know . . . I should've kept my mouth shut . . . I just don't want to see him get hurt anymore."

"He knows that."

Chapter 31

ON SATURDAY, WE ALL GOT READY for the big event. Jack and Wheeler and I put on the tuxedos we'd bought for five dollars apiece at a used-clothing store. Nectarine wore the pants which she'd made herself from a paisley bedspread she'd found in a tree on the edge of town. Even Becky finally agreed to come. She had suggested we leave the kids with Grandma Franklin, but Jack had insisted that grandma come too, so we'd hired a babysitter for the occasion.

Everyone was in good spirits. But I was worried about Jack. I'd noticed a new desperate edge to his tone when he'd announced the event to his class.

At about six o'clock we got ready to leave. Wheeler had loaded his van with the 400 hot headphone radios that Molla had gotten for him at about a third of the usual price. Jack was extremely excited but you could see the shadows under his blazing eyes. He'd been up all night. I'd stood part of the watch with him, outside by the fence. When Millicent's father had moaned, Jack had suggested taking him with us but I talked him out of it.

"OK," Jack said to Wheeler, in our kitchen, "let's go. Do you think the 400 headphones'll be enough?"

"I think so. We can have the people take turns if there's more than 400 there. That way the rest have a chance to watch when they're not dancing."

"Good idea," Jack said. "I put notices on half the telephone poles in the county. And I got some champagne for the victory party here afterwards."

When we went outside to get grandma, Millicent was standing across the way on the edge of the road by herself. She looked lost. Her eyes were red. She had been crying. In the background we could hear her father.

"What's up?" Jack said.

She began to sob. "The building inspectors came today," she said softly. "They condemned our house."

Well, we all just stood frozen there. I didn't know whether to laugh or cry. Then Jack turned to Becky and he said in an angry tone, "You see! You see what I'm up against. And you think *I'm* crazy." He strode away from us in his tuxedo, toward grandma's trailer, saying to no one in particular, "What's *happening* to this country?"

Jack set grandma on a seat in the hatcheck room. He instructed her to take the dollar admission and hand out a pair of earphones to each person who entered. Grandma's face was lit up. She was glad to be allowed to work. Hark stayed there with her. Jack and Wheeler and I brought the hundreds of earphones into the hatcheck room and piled them around grandma. Nectarine and Becky did some last-minute adjustments on the party-like decorations Wheeler and Jack had strung around the hall that morning. The hall seemed like it could hold about 600 people.

A total of twenty-three showed up. Only four of them were in Jack's class. The obese girl, who came with her sister who was even more obese. The guy who went to see "Whacko" the first night. The guy with the natty mustache and his wife, but they only stayed a little while. And stoned-Vince, the Pope and drug man, who was in a sad mood because he said he'd lost his dog.

This other stoned-out young guy we didn't know appeared with no money and a guitar. We let him in for free. He was very short and his hair was dark and stringy and wild. It looked like it had been used to dry-mop the Twenty-third Street station on the Lexington Avenue IRT. He had the beginnings of a scraggly beard. He wanted us to hire him to play the music but when we explained to him what we were doing he just kind of wandered around saying, "I'm not from here. I'm from the city. I'm looking for a gig in the woods, man. A gig in the woods," to every person he met.

Doc Freudenberg was there, and a couple of Wheeler's friends, four drunk high school kids, some of the local hippies, and two crazies—one of whom looked like he'd been on his own private Opteema for several years already, and the other of whom seemed like some kind of speed freak, tall and real thin, wearing a bright green cape. He danced all the time whether the music was on or not, and no matter how often we told him, he kept yelling out, "Shazam!" instead of "Mitzi!" and always at the wrong time.

Most of those who did come were crazy enough to go along with the tap-dancing and Mitzi yelling. For a few songs at least. Jack, of course, danced each dance frantically and we tried to stay with him and help him out as much as we could. But the dancers seemed lost in the large hall. And after a while the high school kids stole off into a dark corner with a bottle of wine and began to get even drunker, and a couple of the hippie guys picked up women and left, and three other folks drifted outside to get loaded with the guy looking for a gig in the woods and didn't return, and two couples began to dance normally to the music, and Vince and the obese sisters took off their earphones and sat on the floor and began to talk about Star Trek.

So all that was left was pretty much our Carmen Miranda Memorial group and the two crazy guys.

For a while, Jack went around to the idlers and encouraged them to join in. He continued to dance madly by himself, and, like I said, we did our best to support him, with even Becky tap-dancing along, but the rest of the people kept dropping out and finally even Jack seemed ready to call it a day.

Doc Freudenberg came up to me. "If he starts dancing again, try to slow him down. He's getting frantic."

"I know . . . I think he's finished, though."

I walked over to Jack. I put my arm around his shoulders. "It wasn't so bad. If you want to be president, remember, you gotta start by eating a lot of chicken dinners in Ohio."

"I know. Thanks."

He walked away and began to collect the headphones. The lack of sleep and a much, much deeper weariness showed on his face. His skin seemed made of paper. He looked, suddenly, like and old man.

It wasn't much of a revolution.

Jack carried grandma back to her trailer. He drank the champagne with us at the house. He was unnaturally quiet. His eyes looked like Howe Caverns before they lit them for the tourists.

When the Doc and Wheeler and Becky left, Nectarine and I tried to cheer him. We put on some of his favorite records. (Best of the Beach Boys, Vol. II, Side 2; Miles Davis at Carnegie Hall, Side 1, with Hank Mobley on tenor, and the great driving rhythm section of Wynton Kelly, Paul Chambers, and Jimmy Cobb; etc.) But he didn't respond.

"Look, Jack, the world's not over," I said. "I've got all these great ideas we can work on. I'm starting a new religion. We believe in the Holy Decimity: The Father, the Son, and the Holy Ghost, the Aunt, the Uncle, the Grandfather, the Grandmother, and the Three Andrews Sisters."

"*The Andrews Sisters?*" Nectarine said.

"Yeah, the Andrews Sisters. Do you remember their names?" She thought for a second.

"Yin and Yang?"

"OK. That's two. Who's the third?"

"Yintz?"

"*Yintz?*"

"I don't know," she champagne-giggled. "It just came into my mind."

I turned back to my brother. "And if that doesn't work, Jack, I've got another idea. An un-health food store for junkies in the city. We'd sell nothing but sodas and sweet stuff and food with preservatives that are bad for you. We'd make a fortune."

But he didn't respond.

He sat there in the big orange chair that Nectarine had gotten for twenty bucks, with his feet on the gold and brown hassock with the stuffing falling out. He continued to drink.

We kept the music going so he wouldn't have to hear Millicent's father.

Finally at 4:00 A.M., he got up, tried to do a Quasimoto imitation, fell over the hassock, and passed out on the floor.

Chapter 32

THE NEXT MORNING Millicent lost control of her car, sheared off our mailbox, ran through our metal wire fence, and killed poor Hark who was sleeping peacefully on our front lawn.

The crash awoke us. I got there first. When I saw that Hark was dying, I rushed to help Millicent out of her car which had slammed into a Douglas fir.

Triage. Leave the dying to save the living. It's amazing how that army experience stays with you.

Jack ran over to Hark and cradled the big dog's helpless head in his lap. Jack wasn't crying. It was clear the big dog was bleeding inside. Bleeding bad. But Jack had been in that position before. With dying men's heads in his lap. After a while, when your work involves watching men die, you learn how to keep from crying. You do your job and you don't let the dying distract you.

I took Millicent back to her house and treated her for basic shock. When I saw she would be OK, I left Nectarine and Jimi with her and went back to my brother. He was seated quietly on the grass next to Hark's body. I was able to get Millicent's car started and drive it back across the road. I borrowed Wheeler's van and backed it up to the broken fence. Jack sat there. I took the spade from Nectarine's garden and the blanket from my brother's bed. I knew he would want me to take the best blanket he had. Then Jack and I gently laid poor

Hark's body onto the blanket in the rear of Wheeler's van.

I got Becky to take Nectarine's place with Millicent, and I drove Jack, Nectarine, and Jimi to the strip of redwood forest that runs between Sebastopol and the ocean.

There was a surprising new chill in the air. A hint that the rainy season would come in sooner than expected. Heavy clouds loomed overhead like theories. The smaller trees shook leaves out of their hair in the wind.

We found a circle of young redwoods around the decapitated stump of the mother tree. We dug a hole nearby, under the protection of the great trees, wrapped the blanket around Hark's body, put him in the hole, and covered him with dirt.

We didn't dance the samba around his grave.

We went to the edge of the continent. We walked slowly along the almost deserted beach. Jack walked ahead of us by himself. Dead jellyfish were strewn about like milky-white electrical insulators.

"Do you ever miss the city?" I asked Nectarine.

"Yeah . . . I guess so . . . I always think of the city as Chicago. I had some good times there . . . "

"You know what I miss? . . . I miss the smell of the *New York Times* at night. Hot off the presses . . . "

She smiled weakly.

"I miss giving directions to tourists," I said. "I really knew the city . . . And I miss listening to other people's conversations in cafeterias."

We walked way up the beach and then Jack turned around and we followed him back. And as we walked along the Pacific coast, I thought of how far from The Bronx we had come. How we were living in exile in our native land. Three thousand miles from the place of our birth. We had gone as far as we could go and still be in America. If we went any further, we would be in the sea.

As we walked up the steps of our porch, we stopped to look at the huge pink Cadillac that floated along our little road. A man was driving. Nectarine's mother, Laura Lee, was seated beside him. The man stopped the car at the gate and rushed out to open Laura Lee's door. He was about sixty years old. And five feet tall. He was wearing a dark blue, Mafia-style, pinstriped suit. He had a pink silk jockey cap on his head.

Laura Lee jauntily led him up to us. She walked through the gate like she was coming on stage in a Broadway musical. "Hello everybody," she said. She kissed Nectarine lightly on the cheek. "I got married again, kids. We just stopped by on our honeymoon. We can only stay a sec." She turned toward the man in the jockey cap which only came up to her shoulder. "This is my new husband, Rodney. He's a jockey."

Rodney took a little bow.

"Is he in a race today or something?" Nectarine said, nodding at his hat.

"No, he's retired. I still have him wear his jockey cap so people won't think he's just another short guy."

Laura Lee noticed the smashed fence. Nectarine told her what had happened. Laura Lee said to Jimi, "Oh . . . Did the big old doggie-woggie get hit by the mean old car?"

"Don't talk that way about my dog." Jack's voice cracked through the crisp air like a gunshot.

Rodney moved in front of Laura Lee. "You can't talk that way to my wife."

"Just don't talk about my dog."

Rodney recognized the tone. There was no mistaking it. And he saw Jack's head, down and still, the way a big dog sets himself when he's ready to bite.

Rodney took Laura Lee's arm and moved her back through the gate. "No one talks that way to my wife, even if he *is* her son-in-law," he said. Then, to Laura Lee, "Come on, honey, let's get out of here."

"Yes, maybe we'd best come back another time," Laura Lee bubbled. "We'll just stop by at mother's for a minute and then be on our merry way. I know how it is. I had dogs myself once."

They got in the Cadillac and continued on up the road to grandma's.

I turned toward Jack. His face looked grim, but there was a steely determination in his eyes. "I've got it. One last chance. I've got it."

He strode into the house.

I felt better. I couldn't worry about what crazy new plan had appeared in his tortured mind. I was just glad to see his eyes light up and his hope return.

Chapter 33

JACK AND WHEELER WERE GONE for five days. No one knew where they were. No one performed the flagpole ceremony. (In fact, the hat was missing.) No one hitched the horse up to Grandma Franklin's mobile home. No one claimed to be Prince Esterhazy and played Mozart out of the windows of the house.

Then on Friday night we got a call. From Jack. All he would tell us was to be at the racetrack at the fairgrounds the following afternoon at three o'clock.

That night Nectarine got a toothache. In the morning, she went to the dentist and he pulled it. She was in great pain. She had to stay home. Becky stayed with her and cared for the kids.

I didn't want to go to the fair alone. I walked over to grandma's. Her TVs were on, but she wasn't there. I wondered where she could be.

I called Doc Freudenberg. We drove out to the fairgrounds together in his Mercedes. We got there at one thirty. It wasn't hard to locate the track. It was the vortex of interest.

To keep my mind off my brother, I bet on the first few races and I lost a couple bucks. The Doc wanted to bet, too. He asked me to explain what "across the board" meant. He bet on a couple races. He won a few bucks.

It was a clear, sunny day. Colorful pennants danced in the wind. The grandstand was crowded. Mostly country folks, picnicking and having a good time. You could tell them by their families. The few city guys who had come up for the day came alone. They were the real gamblers. They looked hungry.

The Doc and I worked our way down to the fence, near the finish line. Just at three o'clock, the fifth race was scheduled to begin. The favorite was a horse called Greenbisquit at 9 to 5. I had five to win on Hugo's Choice. I bet on him on a hunch. I knew I shouldn't have, but when I saw him I couldn't help it. He was easily the most beautiful horse we had seen all day. A big colt with a sleek velvet-black coat and perfect lines, he carried his twelve hundred pounds on long thoroughbred legs as slim as stick-ball bats.

He was a longshot. Going off at 12 to 1. He hadn't finished higher than seventh in any of his last five races. But I noticed that at one point in his career he had won a race in an amazing time. And there was something about him . . . He looked like he didn't belong at a county fair. He seemed much too fine.

Hugo's Choice had the number two post position, but they had trouble getting him into the gate so the race was held up for about four minutes.

When they did start, he broke out into the lead. As they made the clubhouse turn, I heard the sound of a helicopter coming in over the top of the grandstand. There was a large disc-shaped object hanging from it, parallel to the ground, held up by a set of cables from the chopper. It looked like a fake flying saucer. I guess you weren't supposed to see the cables.

"Oh, no . . ."

"What *that?*" the Doc said.

"That's them. Wheeler can fly. He flew with us in Vietnam."

The chopper hovered above the track with the "saucer" below it. The crowd began to buzz. They flocked up to the front, pushing me and the Doc against the shoulder-high fence. Slowly, the chopper lowered the floating saucer, setting it gently down right on the track, over against the inside rail, just up the homestretch from the finish line. The chopper hovered in place overhead. "Hey, what's that?" "What's that?" The crowd grew restless and anxious. "What's that?" "Get it off the track!" "What *is* it?"

The saucer was white, with various dials and meters painted in black on its sides. The top opened. Jack climbed out. He was wearing the Uncle Sam suit that he had worn to his wedding and the Carmen Miranda hat from our flagpole, covered with fresh fruit. With the suit made out of a flag and the hat on top, he looked a little like a flagpole himself. Quickly he moved around the top of the saucer, releasing the cables. When they were all free, the chopper tilted to the side and swung out, fast and low, like we did in Nam, staying just over the tops of the trees to avoid ground fire.

Jack hopped back down into the saucer. The horses came into the far turn. Hugo's Choice was in the lead, neck and neck with Greenbisquit. The crowd was getting more restive.

"He must work for the fair."
"No. He don't."
"Who is he?"
"He *must* be with the fair!"
"What's goin' on?"

Jack climbed out again quickly, like a mad spider, with Grandma Franklin on his back. "Oh, no," I heard myself say. Grandma was holding a bullhorn. He set her down on top of the saucer. She handed the bullhorn to him.

"Hey, get off the track!" an excited fat man shouted at Jack.

"Yeah, get off the track!" his ugly friend yelled.
"What's goin' on?"
"What's happening!"
"Get that fucker off the track!"

"Get off the track!" several people began to shout at him as the horses came around the final turn. "Get off the track!"

Jack put the bullhorn to his mouth and faced the crowd.

"My friends, I want to tell you about another planet. Or another way of looking at the world. I call this the Planet Opteema, where people can accept death and they care for the aged. On this planet people live in harmony and there are no stupid wars . . ."

Then, from the shouts of the crowd, he realized something had gone wrong. He looked to his right. He saw the horses coming at him down the stretch. People continued to shout and to push up toward the front. A woman to my left let out a wild scream of panic. Hugo's Choice and Greenbisquit were way out in the lead. Six or seven lengths at least, dashing madly toward the finish together, Hugo's Choice on the inside. The crowd was excited but stunned into inactivity. They were shouting but there was no time to do anything. The events were happening too quickly for them to comprehend.

Hugo's Choice swung quickly to the right and bumped Greenbisquit as both horses swerved madly to swing outside and around the saucer.

Jack had sick panic in his eyes as he saw what was happening.

SNAP!

The right front leg of Hugo's Choice cracked like a twig in a fireplace. Snap! Somehow, I could swear I heard it. Snap!

Hugo's Choice pulled up short into a hobble. His jockey flew over his head and onto the track. Greenbisquit crossed the line and won the race. The other horses broke stride and veered away from the saucer, clumsily trying to avoid the downed jockey. A redheaded lady to my right fainted, but the crush was so great she couldn't fall at first. People began to scream and curse again at Jack. Men in white and orange groundskeepers' suits ran out onto the track. Jack's face whitened with horror. He began to hobble about in a little circle around grandma, almost in imitation of Hugo's Choice. An ambulance screamed out onto the track and raced toward the fallen jockey. Track attendants ran after the beautiful crippled horse. The fat man next to me climbed over the fence and ran toward Jack. The edge of the saucer top was about five feet off the ground. The fat man struggled like a bloated insect to crawl over it. His ugly friend ran after him and pushed him up onto the flat surface. Jack stepped in front of grandma and threw away the bullhorn. The fat man lunged toward him. Jack grabbed him by the shirt and, using the force of his rush, gave him a kind of judo throw in the same direction. The man seemed to bounce once and then roll off the edge of the saucer and land on the ground on his head and right shoulder. The ugly man took a quick look at Jack's mad face and decided to stay on the ground. He ran over to help his fallen friend.

Jack was frenzied. I could see tears rolling down his face. He darted back and forth on top of the saucer in random, indecisive movements. Then he turned to the cursing crowd and he shouted at them in a desperate, staccato voice, "Please! Please! People of America. It's not too late. We have to forget about Vietnam. We have to go on." A tall man ran onto the track and started up on the saucer. Jack bent down and punched him. The Carmen Miranda hat fell off his head. The tall man toppled back onto the track.

"Please! This is still a free country! We can't just let old people die in ignorance. It's too terrible. Please . . ."

The crowd continued to scream and curse, and they began to throw things at him—beer cups, race programs, anything they could get their hands on. A teenage boy threw his hot dog.

"What's happened to you?" Jack cried, waving his arms wildly in the air. "I *believed* in you." His voice cracked and seemed almost plaintive as he wailed out the grievous cries that tore at me, scarred me with their desperate entreaties, amidst the shouts and flying debris from the crowd.

"You stopped Hitler in World War Two! I believed in you. I loved you. I'm an American. Why can't you help me now?"

I was amazed. He wasn't talking about Opteema at all. I could hardly believe what I was hearing. He seemed to be crooning a last frantic love song, hidden inside a series of pitiful mad-pleading screams that I'll hear every night till the day I die.

"I loved you. When I was a boy you saved the Jews. I'm an American. Why can't you help me now?"

Several people began to climb over the fence at once. Jack scurried to the far side of the saucer. He turned back and wailed at the crowd one last time, "This is still a free country. I'm an American too." Then he leaped off the far side of the saucer, stumbled, regained his balance, and ran wildly across the infield with several members of the mob at his heels.

I leaped over the fence and brought one man down with a flying tackle. We rolled over in the dirt as he tried to punch at me. I guess the crowd continued to curse and scream, but all I could hear was that sad wail of my brother, in his frantic Uncle Sam lament, crying at the people in the stands, "I loved you. When I was a boy, you saved the Jews. I'm an American. Why can't you help me now?"

Chapter
34

THE DOC AND I picked up the pieces as best we could. I wasn't hurt. The guy I tackled had just given me a good kick in the ribs and had taken off after Jack.

We climbed up on the saucer and checked out Grandma Franklin. She was a bit shaken up but she was OK. The jockey that had fallen was badly bruised, but he got up and walked to the ambulance under his own power. Hugo's Choice, however, had to be destroyed.

The Doc lowered grandma down to me on the ground. I put her on my back and carried her to the car. There was still so much confusion that no one thought to stop us to question grandma.

On the way home, I stopped at a gas station to call Nectarine and tell her what had happened. Becky was still there with her. They hadn't heard from Jack or Wheeler.

After we got Grandma Franklin back to her trailer, the Doc and I went over to my house. Nectarine was seated at the kitchen table. The right side of her face was swollen. Her skin looked ashen. The kids were playing quietly in Jimi's room. Becky sat on the floor near the turntable. She was playing a Billie Holiday record softly and sipping a beer.

We sat there for almost an hour, hardly saying a word. Then the phone rang. Nectarine picked it up. *"What?"* she said. "Are you *serious?*" The pain in her face increased. She dropped the phone and silently walked past us into her bedroom, closing the door behind her.

The receiver of the wall phone dangled in the air. I picked it up.

"Hello."

"Jerry?"

"Yeah."

"This is Wheeler. I'm downtown. At the Safeway. Look . . . it's your brother Jack . . . He's locked himself up in Joe Henderson's office . . . over the meat counter . . . The place is full of cops . . . They're gonna break the door in . . ."

"Can you see him? Through that big picture window?"

"Yeah . . . He's got some kind of blackface face on. It must be charcoal or something . . . And he's walking around up there . . . around in circles . . . He won't open the door . . . He seems to be mumbling to himself . . . And his face is twisted and he's all hunched over like . . . kinda like he's doing a Quasimoto imitation . . ."

"Is he laughing, Wheeler? . . . Is it funny?"

"No . . . It's not funny . . . It's not funny at all . . . He's crying his eyes out . . . It's terrible . . . You better get down here. And bring the Doc if he's there . . . It's terrible, Jerry . . . He's walking around in a circle up there like Quasimoto and he's crying . . . It's the saddest thing I've ever seen . . ."

Chapter
35

WELL, THAT'S THE END of the story, I guess. My brother got arrested but the Doc testified at his trial that he had been nuts since he'd been in Vietnam—a kind of service-connected disability—and I got Jack a good lawyer who played up his distinguished war record and his Purple Heart, so the judge pretty much just put him in the Sonoma County Mental Hospital under the Doc's care.

Maybe you read about the case. It was in all the papers. About a year later, the Doc released Jack on probation and he took off and nobody's heard from him since.

But I know he's around. The Doc says he's seen him doing his imitations in bars here in San Francisco. The Doc thinks it's me. He never *could* tell the difference between us.

Nectarine and Jimi and I sold the house after a while, and we moved to a little flat in San Francisco. They call it a railroad flat, but it's so small I think it's really just the station on some rich kid's electric train set. Wheeler and Becky say they're coming down soon to buy a house in the neighborhood and join us.

Grandma Franklin wouldn't leave her mobile home, so I took some of the money we got when we sold the house and I paid to have it towed up to Fort Bragg, a little town up the coast a bit. There's a lot of old people there in mobile homes. We visit her practically every week. She's got a pretty nice setup. The coast is beautiful and you can see the ocean from out her window. I didn't like the idea at first, I wanted her to live with us, but when she insisted, there was nothing I could do.

I live a quiet life here in the city. I do Wheeler's books, and I read and I write most of the time. I walk around the streets a lot. Nectarine likes the used-clothing stores on Mission Street. Jimi's made new friends here. Sometimes he crawls around on all fours and makes believe he's Hark.

Anyhow, I hope you profited from reading this account of our adventures in California.

In closing, all I can say is, if you ever decide to try to build a new world here in America, I wish you the best. I only hope you have better luck than we did.

Oh, yeah, and one last thing. If you run into my brother somewhere, please tell him to come home. Tell him we love him. And we miss him. Things just haven't been the same for us since he's been gone.

You won't have any trouble recognizing him.

He looks a lot like me.